SHATTERED IMAGES

Marcia King-Gamble

SHATTERED IMAGES

sepia™

SHATTERED IMAGES

ISBN-13: 978-1-58314-644-6
ISBN-10:   1-58314-644-X

www.kimanipress.com

Printed in U.S.A.

To my late mother, Cynthia King
and all the unappreciated teachers out there.

A mind is truly a terrible thing to waste.

CHAPTER 1

"'Where the bee sucks, there suck I; in a cowslip's bell I lie...'"

Desiree Alexander sat, eyes closed, enjoying the student's modern-day recitation of *The Tempest*. She was on top of the world. Life simply didn't get much better than this. Here she was, doing what she'd always wanted to do, working with young people and helping shape their minds.

Something must have happened to stop Shakespeare in midsentence. Desiree reluctantly pried open her eyes. She spotted the steel-gray head of Ida, the dean's secretary, peeking through the open door. No wonder there was silence. The students' attention was riveted on Ida.

Ida loudly whispered, "Desiree, Harvey would like to see you." She curved an imperious index finger.

That put an end to order in the classroom. The titters and whispering back and forth began. It was to be expected from sixteen-year-old teenagers, cooped up on a sunny spring day.

"Corinne, I'm putting you in charge," Desiree said to one of her more rambunctious students, a teenager who was extremely bright but preferred not to show it.

Stepping into the narrow hallway, Desiree huffed out a sigh. "What's so urgent that Harvey needs to interrupt my class?"

Ida shrugged and rolled her eyes. She was a gaunt woman with a tendency to overexaggeration. "Beats me. Mr. Coleman simply told me to find you wherever you were. I wasn't about to argue with him."

It had to be serious or Harvey would have waited until her class ended. Desiree glanced at her Movado watch, realizing that would be in less than half an hour. Surely whatever it was could have been dealt with then.

Her high-heeled pumps sinking into the plush carpeting, a slightly irritated Desiree followed Ida up the hallway and toward Harvey's palatial office, otherwise known as The Rack. More often than not, one teacher or another was summoned there to be grilled.

As the door shut behind her, the dean waved her to an overstuffed chair. "Have a seat, Desiree. I'll try to keep this brief."

Brief or not, Desiree didn't have time to sit. She needed to get back to her class before things got totally out of control.

"What is it, Harvey?" Desiree asked, remaining standing.

Harvey Coleman laced his fingers together and peered at Desiree over half-moon glasses. "I'll need your resignation letter on my desk by close of business today."

Desiree blinked at him. He couldn't be serious. On the other hand she'd never known Harvey to be a joker.

"What's this about, Harvey?" she asked, trying not to let her irritation show. "I'm in the middle of teaching a class. You wouldn't want to keep the future leaders of tomorrow waiting."

Harvey didn't so much as blink an eyelash. "I will expect your resignation by the end of today. We'll pay you through the school term, of course."

"What?" He still wasn't making sense. "This is nonsense. Are you laying me off? Are things really that bad? Come on, Harvey, you could have asked for wage concessions. I would have bit."

Harvey cleared his throat and set down his expensive pen on the desk.

"Desiree, this has nothing to do with the school's financial situation or the economy. It has to do solely with you."

"Me?" Shock was slowly taking hold. "Last week you were telling me how terrific I was with the kids. You felt confident I could step into your shoes and do more than an adequate job. You pretty much confirmed that I would be the first female dean of Fannie Jackson. What happened between last week and now to make me fall out of favor?"

Harvey yanked open a drawer of the gigantic mahogany desk and removed what looked to be a video.

"This!" he said, slamming down the case in front of her. "This Desiree, this. Viewing this filth still has my stomach churning."

Desiree's own stomach flip-flopped. No, it couldn't possibly be. But even as she dismissed the thought as preposterous, the image of a desperate young girl flashed through her mind. Why now, after all these years of respectable living, had her past come back to haunt her?

What should matter was the number of kids who graduated her English classes with a 4.0 cumulative average, the students that had almost perfect SAT scores, and the growing numbers that went on to receive Ivy League educations, not some indiscretion from her youth.

"Speak to me in English," Desiree snapped, bluffing. "What does a videotape have to do with this discussion? And with me being fired? What could be on that tape that's so incriminating?"

Harvey looked at her like he'd just swallowed something sour. He reclaimed his seat, opting for the safety of a barrier between them. He reached for a folder, which Desiree realized had her name on it, flipped it open, and removed a thick sheaf of paper.

"Do you remember this?" Harvey thrust a wad of papers at her.

"What is that?"

"The business ethics disclosure you signed."

Desiree frowned. This whole thing was simply bizarre.

When she remained silent, Harvey continued, "By signing these papers you agreed nothing you said or did would compromise the school's good name."

"Yes, that's true."

"Fannie Jackson has been compromised."

For the second time, Desiree's stomach lurched. The skin on the back of her neck actually prickled. No it wasn't possible…that video had been taken a long time ago. Almost twenty years…another life. Another time and she'd been under the impression it had been destroyed.

"What's on that tape?" Desiree challenged, wanting Harvey to confirm her suspicions.

This time Harvey had difficulty meeting her eyes.

"I'm sure you know and I'm equally sure you understand why our association has to end. For what it's worth, I've enjoyed working with you, Desiree." He extended his ebony hand as though he fully expected her to shake it. Desiree let his hand dangle in midair. Harvey shoved it back into his jacket pocket. "You're a terrific teacher and a gifted one," he said, as if that were supposed to make her feel better.

After what could only be described as an awkward moment, Harvey handed Desiree the tape.

"Take this," he said. "View it in the privacy of your home. I've got another copy. Your check can be sent to any address you designate."

Desiree took the video from him. There really wasn't

much else to do. Her manicured hand tugged on the collar of the tailored shirt she wore under her suit jacket. "This stinks, Harvey," she eventually said. "Really stinks. You haven't heard or seen the last of me."

Harvey actually deigned to step out from behind his desk. Taking Desiree by the elbow, he edged her toward the door. "If you need anything," he said, his voice lowering an octave, "don't hesitate to call. Good luck to you."

"I need my job," Desiree practically shouted, as Harvey's other hand circled the brass knob of the closed office door.

"That I can't help you with."

"I have every intention of taking this to the school board," she warned. "Like I said before, I will not go quietly."

Harvey paused, his hand still on the knob.

"That would not be a good idea. The fewer people brought into this, the better off you'll be."

Desiree's head was spinning. She felt as if all the wind had been knocked out of her. "Are you threatening me?" she asked.

"Not threatening, just advising you not to risk the bad publicity. Look at the tape first before you determine any course of action."

Harvey turned the doorknob and stood aside. In a daze, Desiree walked out, ignoring Ida, who had probably been eavesdropping.

She managed somehow to put one foot in front of the

other and make it down the hallway without once stopping to admire Lee White's art adorning the walls. This afternoon she was in no mood to appreciate the renditions of America's foremost black artist.

As she continued on her way, she passed a number of colleagues leaving their classrooms. Desiree managed to nod in their direction and hurried on. Was it her imagination or was she being given curious looks? At the age of thirty-seven, and after eight years of giving her all to a fine black institution, she was without a job.

She needed to get home and think things through. But first she would stop by her office and get her purse. Packing would have to wait for another day when her stomach had settled and she was up to being questioned by colleagues and friends. Most would find it strange that she of all people, Ms. Dedication, was leaving in the middle of the spring term. And, yes, her abrupt ousting would make sense if the secret she'd carried all these years had been exposed.

Desiree's office was as she'd left it: assignments still to be graded strewn across the glass-topped desk; a pair of comfortable Chinese slippers discarded in the corner; a stack of books, mostly classics, piled on the chintz-covered sofa; the mug of tea she'd been sipping on earlier, left to grow cold.

Her burning brown eyes now focused on a crystal vase as Desiree toyed with taking home the roses Byron, her boyfriend, had sent her only yesterday. They were all in full bloom.

Still needing a moment to gather her wits, she collapsed into the leather swivel chair and massaged her throbbing temples. The perfumed scents of an early spring floated through the open window, almost making her gag. The sounds of a sputtering lawn mower now wreaked havoc with the war in her head. Desiree got up and slammed the window shut.

After a while, she yanked open the bottom drawer of the desk and grabbed her purse, stuffing the video into it. A knock on the office door now got her attention. Bad timing, whoever it was.

A dreadlocked head poked in to the opening as a nut-brown face with a million-dollar smile called a cheery greeting.

"Hey, Desi. You're supposed to be developing young minds, not playing hooky."

Zinga's lighthearted ribbing indicated she didn't have an inkling of what had gone on. Harvey had done a good job of keeping her firing under wraps, at least for now. For a fleeting moment Desiree actually considered inviting her friend and colleague in. She could use a shoulder to cry on, but Byron's would have to do. He'd indicated yesterday he was cutting his trip short and would be home earlier than planned.

Desiree tossed a half-hearted smile at Zinga, one that apparently told the woman everything she needed to know.

"Got it!" the perky, petite teacher in the kente cloth outfit said. "Now is not the time. Call me later."

"I will."

A half hour went by before Desiree opened the door to her condominium. She'd scrimped and saved to come up with the huge down payment, no easy feat for a woman who'd never been thrifty. But at least it was her own.

Like many single women, Desiree spent almost everything she earned. Having her own home had been important to her and she'd recently taken out a huge loan to redo the kitchen. Those renovations were currently underway.

Desiree had hoped that her single status would have changed by now. She'd been dating Byron Fisher, a corporate attorney, for going on three years—heck, they practically lived together—but Byron was dragging his feet.

"Byron," Desiree called as she entered the stark living room that she'd been too busy to decorate.

The silence greeting her meant only one thing—Byron's plane had been delayed. Desiree's skull felt as if nails were being hammered into it as she made her way to the kitchen. She tossed her purse and the damn video on the counter, swallowed two aspirins, and microwaved water for tea.

Next on the agenda would be watching that video, and she should do it before Byron arrived. If the tape contained what she suspected, she'd have to decide how best to break the news. Byron would not take the revelation well.

In stocking feet, and feeling exceedingly vulnerable, Desiree plunked the video in the player, then flopped onto the leather couch, the sole piece of furniture in the living room, except for the television. With some trepidation, she pressed the remote button and waited for the tape to begin.

Please, God, let Byron not arrive in the middle of this.

The screen flickered and then grew fuzzy. It looked as if it was snowing. The camera slowly focused in. Desiree distinctly saw two forms now; one was a man, the other a woman with a wild head of hair. Both were totally nude. The man was caressing the woman's copper body, touching her in the most intimate of places, and the woman was touching him back. When the female got on her knees and took the man in her mouth, Desiree stabbed the button, stopping the film midway.

"Oh, God, how could I have done this?" she said, covering her mouth.

The tape had brought back memories of a difficult time. It was a vivid and sordid reminder of how desperate she'd once been.

CHAPTER 2

The shrill ringing of the phone brought Desiree back to the present.

"I just heard the news," Zinga said the moment Desiree picked up. "All sorts of rumors are flying. I thought, why not hear it from the source?"

Bad news did travel fast. "What have you heard?" Desiree asked, fearing she already knew the answer.

"Just that you and Harvey had a big argument and you walked out. There's speculation that you didn't get the job. It's BS, right?"

It would only be a matter of time before the real truth got out. Should she tell Zinga what had really happened or should she keep the situation to herself?

Desiree had no idea how her friend would react. She'd

never told anyone at Fannie Jackson that at the age of seventeen she'd been a runaway and desperate for money. She'd never let it slip that she came from a well-respected Atlanta family with a father who ranked right up there with Dr. Martin Luther King.

She'd actually been ashamed to admit that her father, a respected and dynamic civil rights leader, a staunch supporter of the cause, had two faces. The public one he showed to the world, the private one only his family saw. He was not the devoted family man everyone thought he was. In reality, he was a womanizer who disrespected his wife and family with his constant philandering.

"Des, are you there?" Zinga's voice brought her back to the present.

"I'm here."

"Want to talk or should I call back later?"

"No. It's okay. We can talk."

"Well, is it true? Did you really tell Harvey to get lost?"

"Not exactly. It was more the other way around."

Zinga's breath came through the earpiece in little puffs. How much should she tell her?

"Harvey decided I didn't suit the Fannie Jackson image," Desiree said, settling for an abbreviated version.

"Now, *that's* BS. You're one of the classiest people I know."

"That's a matter of opinion. Harvey doesn't think so. He found out about something I did a long time ago."

Zinga waited, her silence indicating she was struggling to understand.

How did she tell her friend that her life as a teenager had been so unbearable that she'd packed up her bags and taken off? That to cope she often created a fantasy world? Acting had seemed the answer, though it was a profession her father thought beneath her. His highbrow associates in Atlanta would think less of him if she didn't follow in his footsteps and get a law degree. They'd had a huge argument and she'd packed the bare minimum and escaped.

"I did something foolish when I was a teenager," Desiree admitted. "I accepted a job I should never have taken and Harvey found out about it."

"Come on, whatever it is couldn't be that bad," Zinga answered compassionately.

"It's pretty awful. I couldn't even deny it. Harvey had the evidence in his office."

"Oh, boy. But why now? Why did whatever it is take so long to surface?"

That was something Desiree had asked herself. How on earth had Harvey gotten hold of that tape? And why, after all of these years, had it suddenly appeared? Someone clearly wanted her out of the way. Who was that someone?

After giving it some thought, the conclusion she'd come to wasn't a pretty one. It had to be one of the candidates after Harvey's job. There were only three she knew of.

Visiting history professor Rafiq Jones had tossed his hat in the ring, claiming he was seeking permanency. Then there was math teacher Phyllis Wright, one of the few Caucasians on staff. She'd been around forever and ever. Phyllis had integrated Fannie Jackson, or so she claimed. Last was an outside candidate whose name no one knew.

When Desiree remained silent Zinga said, "So Harvey fired you?"

"I was asked to resign."

"Now, that's not right."

Saying it made it suddenly real and the enormity of it all hit her. She was fired and out in the cold. Desiree felt the tears coming, but refused to give in to that small indulgence. She resisted the urge to pound her fists against the walls and bang her head against the huge refrigerator. Her job at Fannie Jackson had meant everything to her.

"You're a wonderful teacher," Zinga said. "Harvey Coleman is a fool to let you go."

"Thanks for the vote of confidence."

She *was* a wonderful teacher. Years ago she'd stumbled into a profession that was tailor-made for her. Desiree had developed an uncanny ability to connect with young people. She sought to make a difference in young people's lives, seeing it as her duty to set them on the right path and assure them a future. If nothing else, it helped assuage her guilt.

"If I can do anything," Zinga offered, "anything at all, let me know. I'll even talk to Harvey on your behalf."

"Thanks, but I don't think it would make a difference."

It wouldn't. That blasted video had ruined everything. It had already thrown her well-ordered life into turmoil and shattered her safe little world.

"I'll let you go, then. Your head must be whirling," Zinga said. "You know where I am if you need me."

Desiree hung up. Since moving to Bethesda she'd made one good friend. Even so, Zinga probably could never understand what desperation could make a person do. In this case, it had driven her to make a film she wasn't proud of. And it wasn't as if she'd been paid a fortune, either. The project had been scrapped.

She'd been stupid not to get something in writing that assured her that tape would be destroyed. But at seventeen, she'd been naive and trusting. Yes, she'd been a total fool.

It was too late; the damage had already been done. Time to put on her sweats and go for a run. Fresh air and pushing her muscles to the limit might help clear her thoughts. At any rate, it would calm her down. She'd come up with a plan. Desiree doubted she would find a job locally. Word would get out and she doubted Harvey's supposed benevolence would extend to providing references.

The moment Desiree entered her bedroom, she knew Byron had been there. She could smell the subtle scent of his musky cologne in the air. The closet doors were wide open and she didn't remember leaving them that way. For a second she thought she'd been robbed, but a cursory check of her valuables assured her she was off base. Besides, she had an alarm code only she and Byron knew.

She crossed over to the closet to shut the doors and noticed one half of the closet was empty. Byron's side. His sweats, a couple of shirts and his forest-green bathrobe were missing. His shoes were gone, too: a pair of sneakers and the Cole Haan loafers he wore when they went out. Her heart pounding, Desiree decided not to jump to conclusions. Then she spotted an envelope propped up on her pillow and she knew.

Desiree gulped air as the world spun around her. With a shaking hand she slid a nail under the flap of the envelope and withdrew Byron's monogrammed stationery. She read his words hastily. Excuses and apologies did not make up for the two brutal words that summed it all up: *It's over*.

Byron had dumped her.

It was way too much for one person to handle. With a choking sob, Desiree collapsed in a fetal position and let the tears flow.

When the phone rang, she considered not answering it. But then she thought it might be Byron. What if he'd decided he'd made a mistake? In the past he'd always been supportive and trustworthy. Despite whatever issues they'd had, he'd always been there for her.

Desiree picked up the receiver. "Byron, is that you?"

"Wrong, girlfriend. It's Sandi."

Sandi who? She knew at least three. Better to let the caller speak and she'd eventually figure it out.

"How soon we forget," the Sandi on the other end said smoothly. Desiree was slowly getting the voice. "It's your old roommate and supposed best friend. I didn't expect to find you home at this hour. I expected to have to leave a message on your machine."

She must want something. Desiree forced enthusiasm into her voice when she answered. "Sandi Thomas? Is that really you? When did you get back from Amsterdam?"

"A few days ago. I'm in New York staying at some overpriced hotel."

Strange that this Sandi would choose today of all days to call. It had been ages since they'd talked, though they maintained an e-mail connection. But Sandi hadn't once mentioned returning to the United States.

As was her habit, Sandi continued a nonstop stream of babble. Her stories were distracting enough to almost make Desiree forget her current worries.

"I've decided to make the U.S. home base for a while and I'll need a place to stay," Sandi said, as effusive as ever. "So I was thinking—you have this huge condo I could move into. I'd pay you rent, of course."

Stunned, Desiree couldn't think of a thing to say. It was just like Sandi to assume that she would go along with her plans. Sandi knew she wouldn't dare turn her down.

Couldn't. Still, having a roommate could very well be the answer to her worries: how to pay the mortgage when there was no longer a paycheck coming in; and how to continue her kitchen renovations. But every caution button lit up. Why would Sandi leave Amsterdam where she was a successful actress to return to the United States? A country she professed to hate?

"So what do you think about us being roomies again?" Sandi asked cheerfully.

Desiree's stomach roiled. She'd gone that route before. As grateful as she'd been to have a place to live, living with the actress hadn't been all laughs. The woman had some irksome habits and was insensitive to other people's needs. Sandi lived life in the fast lane. It was a life so drama-filled Desiree could barely keep up.

"Let me think about it," Desiree said. "Give me a number and I'll get back to you."

"What's there to think about, hon? You owe me."

Desiree supposed she did. But would that debt ever be paid off?

Sandi was still talking a mile a minute, repeating her international cell phone number and urging Desiree to write it down. "How's the man?" she asked.

"Which man?"

"Your Byron. You've been seeing him for quite some time."

"Okay, I guess."

"You guess?"

Sandi didn't need to know there were problems, not until Desiree had spoken with Byron herself.

"You know men," Desiree said, keeping it vague and noncommittal. "They run hot and cold."

Sandi heaved out a sigh. "Do I ever."

After listening to another long-winded monologue, Desiree finally got Sandi off the phone.

Coming to a sudden decision, Desiree decided she wouldn't let Byron get away with his cowardly act. She'd confront him and force him to talk to her, right after she took her run.

An hour later, Desiree climbed out of the shower and began to dress. Running had helped take a bit of the edge off, but not enough.

She was not looking forward to the upcoming confrontation but it needed to be done. After almost three years of dating, Byron owed her an explanation. Desiree strongly suspected there might be a woman involved. Men usually did not sever relationships unless a backup waited in the wings.

She was in her SUV and heading for Byron's elegant town house ten minutes later.

As Desiree pulled up, she noted Byron's Lexus parked in the driveway. She tromped up the walkway, mounted three little steps and without knocking, inserted her key in the lock.

"Is somebody out there?" Byron's voice called from the vicinity of his bedroom.

Desiree's intuition told her to keep quiet. She crept up the hallway, hearing the sounds of frantic rustling and whispered voices. Clearly Byron was not alone.

She stood in front of the closed bedroom door steeling herself for what she would find. Should she enter unannounced? Byron was clearly two-timing her, and dammit if that didn't hurt. How long had this been going on? How many people knew?

As she stood figuring out how to handle this, the bedroom door opened and a half-dressed Byron emerged, buttoning up his shirt.

"Desiree, what are you doing here? Didn't you get my note?"

He appeared flustered and unsure, far from the cool, collected, sophisticated man she knew.

"Yes, I got your note. And that's why I'm here. We need to talk."

She could swear there was sweat on his brow. He grabbed her arm and began propelling her back the way she'd come. "That's not a good idea. How about we set up a date?"

Desiree held her ground. She turned, glaring at him. "How about we talk now."

"Byron, honey, who are you talking to?" a woman's husky voice called from the bedroom.

"Uh, a friend stopped by. Nothing to worry about."

Desiree tugged out of his reach. She was about to make her presence known.

"A friend has your key?" the woman said, sounding leery. "Send whoever it is away and come back to bed."

"Easier said than done," Desiree said, pushing by Byron and stomping up the hallway. She entered the bedroom.

"Please, Desiree," Byron pleaded from behind her. "Don't embarrass yourself."

"You started it," Desiree reminded him, her eyes spilling over with tears as she took in the scene. This was the bedroom she'd decorated, the bed she'd slept in.

A woman with skin the color of a Reeses's Peanut Butter Cup sat up in bed, clutching the covers. She eyed Desiree, the unwanted intruder with distaste. "How did you get into the house?" she demanded.

Desiree waved her key at her. "I have a key. I've had a key for years."

"You're the ex-girlfriend," the woman said. "Poor little thing. Byron should have gotten his key back when he dumped you."

How humiliating. This woman knew. They'd planned it together, yet she'd been so blind she hadn't even seen it coming. It took every ounce of restraint for Desiree not to lunge at her. She wanted to rip off the sheets and tear out the woman's eyes. But she would not give either Byron or his woman the satisfaction of seeing her lose her dignity.

She turned and flung the house key at Byron. "Bastard!"

"Okay, okay, that's enough," Byron said, grabbing her by the shoulders and turning her back the way she had come. "You'd better leave."

"Get your hands off me."

She was at the door. The tears had subsided and all that remained was an enormous pain that settled in her chest. "For the record, you jerk," she gulped, turning back, "you're not much of a man. What a crummy way to end a relationship."

"I'm sorry, Desiree," Byron said, sounding as if he might even mean it.

"Not as sorry as I am."

Desiree slammed his front door.

She was halfway home when she indulged in her third cry of the day.

Disaster supposedly came in threes. And so far they were right on target. She'd been fired, cheated on, and now her worst nightmare, the friend who was really not a friend, would be back in town.

Could life get any worse?

CHAPTER 3

"Something doesn't sound right," Rafiq said, balancing the cordless phone between his ear and shoulder. All the while his eyes were on the blinking monitor. His mind was still on the work he'd been in the midst of before Phyllis called.

"The field is now wide open for us," Phyllis chuckled. "Oh, what I would have given to see Harvey Coleman's expression."

"But why would Desiree Alexander just walk out on a budding career?" Rafiq said absentmindedly. "She had everything going for her."

"Could be she didn't leave of her own volition." Another chuckle punctuated the bomb she'd just delivered. "I'll call around and see what I can find out. We'll catch up later. Meanwhile, you keep your ear to the ground."

Rafiq Jones hung up the phone thinking that something just didn't add up. Desiree Alexander wouldn't just chuck a decent job at Fannie Jackson unless there was something else pending.

He viewed the news Phyllis Wright had just shared with mixed feelings. He *should* be ecstatic. Desiree had been his rival. Everyone thought she was a shoo-in for the position and definitely the woman to watch.

Rafiq was the visiting history instructor at Fannie Jackson, a position that would cease to exist when the semester ended. He needed this job badly. In many ways it had been a lifesaver. It had kept him on the straight and narrow.

Rafiq had been banging away at his computer, working on his great American novel, when the phone rang. Not particularly pleased at the interruption, he'd gruffly answered only to find Phyllis Wright, math teacher and resident Fannie Jackson gossip, on the other end. Phyllis was not one of his favorite people.

That she was a candidate for Harvey Coleman's position was beside the point. Rafiq strongly suspected she'd thrown her hat in the ring so that she could howl loudly that she'd been discriminated against if she was passed over. Phyllis was the only white contender Rafiq knew of.

The minute he'd picked up the phone Phyllis had started in, rambling on about Desiree's sudden departure. She'd made it clear she suspected Desiree might not have left of her own accord.

Why would a committed, well-respected teacher up

and leave? The whole thing was puzzling. Teachers like Desiree Alexander didn't burn bridges and quit good teaching posts. They gave notice, received farewell parties and said proper goodbyes.

Maybe he should call Desiree and find out what was going on. They weren't exactly friends, but it wouldn't hurt for one colleague to check on another.

Rafiq searched through a desk drawer and found the teachers' directory. He dialed Desiree's number and waited for someone to pick up. He was sure there was more to this story. Desiree's hasty departure was not in keeping with the dedicated, elegant woman he'd met.

The phone rang for what seemed an eternity. Finally someone answered.

"Hello."

The voice was female and very husky. Rafiq wondered if he'd woken whoever it was up.

"Desiree Alexander, please."

"This is she."

"Desiree, this is Rafiq Jones. I heard you resigned and I wanted to let you know how much I enjoyed working with you. Had I known you were leaving I would have liked to have taken you to lunch."

There was a pause on the other end, and then finally, "It's thoughtful of you to call, Rafiq. Actually, very nice of you."

Her voice sounded mechanical, as if she were going through the motions. Rafiq sensed her distress and wished he could do something.

"Did you accept a position at another school?" he pried. "I'd been looking forward to you giving me a run for my money. You were a formidable opponent."

Another pregnant pause followed.

"I was fired," Desiree finally admitted. "I didn't leave on my own."

"Fired!" Rafiq parroted. "Impossible!" Phyllis Wright had alluded to something like this but, given her penchant for exaggeration, he hadn't believed her. What could Desiree have done to warrant termination? As a teacher with a long-standing history of excellence, she basically had it made.

"That's the long and short of it," Desiree continued, sighing. "I was let go."

"May I ask what happened?"

He was pushing their professional relationship to the limit. The circumstances weren't his business. He hadn't developed the type of relationship with Desiree that inspired confidences. But she sounded so hopeless his heart went out to her.

"It's a rather long and sordid story," Desiree answered, sounding as if she might have been shedding a tear or two.

"Tell you what, hold on to the story. How about I take you out for a drink?"

The invitation was an impulsive one, but Rafiq figured Desiree needed a distraction, and maybe getting her out of her house would provide that. His ex-colleague sounded as if she needed a solid shoulder to lean on, and if nothing else, he could offer her one.

Rafiq had always viewed Desiree as the model of composure. He'd admired how she remained cool, calm and collected during challenging teachers' meetings. Some had even accused her of being cold and remote. Maybe that was because she wasn't one to hang out afterward and gossip. She usually did her thing and went home.

A beat went by, then another. Rafiq thought that Desiree might be considering how to graciously turn him down.

"Sure I'll join you for a drink. And thank you," she said. "I'll probably have more than one."

He realized he was actually delighted that she'd agreed. "How about we meet at Senor Grogg's in an hour? Is that enough time?" he asked before she could change her mind.

"Yes, I can make it in an hour. See you there."

Rafiq had chosen Senor Grogg's because it was a local hangout and fairly close by. It drew a neighborhood crowd of mostly professionals and was the kind of establishment that didn't require dressing up.

After hanging up, he headed for the shower. He wanted Harvey Coleman's position badly but was sorry Desiree had been disqualified. He couldn't imagine what she could have done to deserve immediate dismissal. Had she changed a student's grades? Acted in an inappropriate manner? Either seemed out of character for the woman he knew.

His sympathy was definitely with her. Not too long ago he was out of work and feeling as if his life had ended. The period after his divorce had been a particularly dismal one. He'd not only ended a marriage but also lost a child. His concentration was off and he'd found himself floundering. He'd merely existed, putting one foot in front of the other. And, finally, he'd applied for a leave of absence and had been turned down. So, opting for sanity, he'd simply quit.

Rafiq had sold the few items left from his divorce settlement and gone off on a two-year trek through Africa. It had turned out to be one of the most therapeutic and educational experiences of his life. And during that time of healing he'd made up his mind to write a novel that would chronicle his life.

Now he went about the business of dressing, trying to decide what to wear. Normally it took him no time to get ready; a jogging suit and sneakers didn't require thought. But tonight he opted for pressed chinos and a freshly laundered shirt before stepping into the stylish loafers he wore to work. After a quick glance in the mirror, he shrugged on a leather bomber jacket and headed out.

Deciding not to take his car because it was a nice night, he sauntered up the avenue. The ten-minute walk took double the usual time. He was dragging his feet and he didn't know why. He stopped to gaze at the windows of the swanky shops, not that there was anything that particularly interested him. He'd said he'd meet Desiree in an hour; waiting in a loud bar just wasn't his thing.

Finally he came to a stop in front of the bright orange striped awning of the building that housed Senor Groggs. The tables and chairs on the sidewalk were spilling over with people chatting up a storm.

Giving a quick glance around to ensure Desiree was not in the chattering crowd, Rafiq entered the wood-paneled foyer. He hurried toward a harried-looking hostess surrounded by patrons, pausing as he spotted Desiree rushing in.

She wasn't at all the totally pulled-together woman he remembered. Her hair was no longer in its neat little bun but flowed behind her. Her trench coat flapped open, the belt trailing from a solitary tab. Under her coat she wore jeans and a red V-necked sweater.

The whole effect was one of a slightly windblown woman who'd pulled on clothes and left her house hastily. Yet she was still one of the most attractive women in the place.

Ignoring the hand she extended, he gave her a quick hug.

"Hey, you. You look great."

She seemed taken back by his greeting but managed a watery smile in return.

"Am I late?" she asked.

"Not at all."

Rafiq held Desiree by the elbow and ushered her into the line of waiting people.

"Is it just you two?" the hostess asked, scanning the monitor of a computer.

"Yes, it's just us."

"Okay, I may be able to seat you."

The people waiting their turn groaned. The groaning grew louder when the hostess stepped out from behind the podium and said, "Follow me."

Still holding onto Desiree's elbow, Rafiq followed the hostess to the back of the room. They were seated at a tiny table for two.

An awkward moment followed. With the exception of faculty meetings, they had not spent much time together before.

"So tell me," Rafiq began, breaking what was starting to be an uncomfortable silence. "What's this about you being fired? Is this someone's idea of a sick joke?"

Desiree hung her coat over the back of the chair. She tugged at the neckline of her sweater while Rafiq tried not to stare. The sweater hugged all the right places and red did wonders for her coppery skin. Rafiq forced himself to look her in the face; a face with perfectly chiseled features and a nose that flared.

Desiree's almond-shaped brown eyes met his gaze head on. While some might consider her mouth too wide, Rafiq thought her lips were perfect. He could easily get lost in her smile.

She was far from the calm woman she usually was tonight. Desiree's fingers toyed with the starched burgundy napkin that peeked from the wineglass. She looked like she needed a drink.

"I'm going to find someone," Rafiq said, rising and giving her time to gather her composure.

At that moment a waitress materialized.

Rafiq took his seat again.

"What can I get you?" the young woman asked, pad already open.

"Desiree?" Rafiq slanted her a look.

"A glass of red wine will be fine."

"Mondavi for the lady. I'll have a cup of coffee, black."

His choices produced another watery smile. "I must look like I need the entire bottle. You're only having coffee."

"I don't drink alcohol." He sounded curter than he intended.

They could barely hear themselves. The place was overflowing with people and the mostly African-American and Latin patrons seemed to be having a good time. In the background, piano keys tinkled while a jazz musician held his own.

Their waitress was back very quickly. She set down Rafiq's cup, handed Desiree her wine, then slapped down menus.

"How about we split an appetizer?" Rafiq offered. "Chicken quesadillas or chips and salsa sound good to you?"

"Either."

He'd suggested appetizers because he sensed Desiree had probably not had dinner. After placing their order, he clinked his cup against her glass. "To good health, eternal happiness and a long, long life. Now tell me the whole story from the beginning."

Desiree held her wineglass, staring into the burgundy contents as if it held insight into her future. Finally she said, "A mistake I made a long time ago came back to haunt me."

"I can't imagine you doing anything so bad it would affect you now."

"You'd be surprised. I've had quite the past."

"Everyone has a past."

His he sometimes didn't want to think about.

Desiree sighed. "It was something I did when I was young and not terribly bright."

"Would it help to talk about it?"

Desiree chuckled deprecatingly. "It's not something I'm especially proud of."

Regrets. He certainly had a few of his own. Now was not the time to take them out for examination. This conversation was not about him. The woman sitting across from him was obviously hurting. He would listen if she cared to talk.

"Is there anything you can do to get your job back?" Rafiq asked, switching the topic. "Maybe there's something I can do. I'd be willing to speak with Harvey if you think that would help."

Desiree took another sip of wine. "That's a very kind offer but speaking with Harvey won't help. I created my own mess and my only choice is to look for another job outside of the Bethesda area." She sighed loudly. "Why are you being so nice? We barely know each other. You've got a good shot at Harvey's job now."

Good question. Why was he being so nice? "We're colleagues," Rafiq answered, "and it seems you could use a friend." He held his breath. Would she accept his explanation or question it further?

He felt sorry for her. Desiree had always come across as a confident woman. Now she seemed as if her world had shattered. He'd been there once. It wasn't a good place to be.

"Friends aren't that easy to find."

It was a strange response. "Don't you have a boyfriend? Would he move with you if you found something out of state? It's hard relocating to a new area without some support."

"You did it."

"True."

Rafiq had heard something about a boyfriend, and at times he'd seen her get out of a midnight-blue Lexus in front of the school.

"That's over," she answered, draining the last of her glass.

What could he say? Offer some silly platitude? He was thinking of doing just that when another teacher came bounding over.

"Desiree," she said, ignoring him totally and throwing her arms around Desiree's shoulders. "I didn't expect to find you here."

"I didn't expect to be here."

Rafiq vaguely remembered the woman's name—Zing: something or other. She taught French. She'd never made much time for him. Her greeting was so effusive she drew the attention of those at the neighboring tables.

"Would you like to sit?" Rafiq asked, more out of courtesy than a desire to have Zinga join them.

"I'm meeting some people, none of whom have shown." Zinga looked him over as if not sure what to make of the situation. "You two are friends?" Her honey-blond locks swung back and forth. "Where's Byron?"

Byron was the boyfriend, of course.

"I have no idea where Byron is," Desiree answered. She gestured to a vacant chair nearby. "Why don't you pull that over here and sit?"

"Yes, please," Rafiq repeated, having no choice but to pretend to be pleased. Catching the eye of the waitress, he signaled for another glass of wine.

Zinga was busy yakking away, her dreadlocks bouncing.

"There's more gossip, girl—people are saying someone sent Harvey nude photos of you!"

"People are wrong. It was an incriminating video," Desiree admitted, sounding like her whole world was on the verge of collapsing.

Rafiq kept his expression neutral but his ears open. Never in his wildest imaginations had he expected something like this. The story reminded him of another scandal in which a beautiful, accomplished woman had made a disastrous choice.

"I made a movie when I was seventeen years old and trying to break into show business," Desiree said, her voice catching. "I didn't even know that video was still around."

"An X-rated movie? Lordie, child, didn't you have better sense?"

Desiree looked as if she were about to crumble. Rafiq's heart reached out to her. Yet she said nothing to defend herself.

Zinga's eyes grew even wider as she settled more comfortably into her chair. "I'll ask this again. Why would someone send Harvey an old video of you? What do they have to gain?"

Desiree just groaned. "Who knows? They had their reasons, I suppose."

"It seems obvious to me," Zinga said, looking directly at him. "It was someone after Harvey's job. Someone desperate enough to want to sabotage you." She gave another sideways glance at Rafiq. God, how he wanted to throttle the woman.

It didn't take a rocket scientist to figure out Zinga thought he was the villain. Desiree was probably thinking the same thing, and who could blame her?

There was little he could do to defend himself, except sit and take it; neither of them would really believe he'd never stoop that low. Rafiq sat stewing for what easily had to be half an hour while the two of them talked.

Eventually Zinga's friends showed up and she departed. The rapport they'd enjoyed previously was now gone. All in all, it had been an awful night. Rising, Rafiq tossed a handful of bills on the table.

"Shall we head out?"

"I suppose."

Desiree accepted the hand he held out and woodenly walked with him to the door.

He knew what it was like to be down-and-out and all he'd been doing was trying to help.

CHAPTER 4

Rain pelted the glass panes of the spacious living room. Desiree gazed out onto a lawn that was slowly making the transformation from yellow to green. The few people out and about were struggling with umbrellas and looked as if they might be blown off their feet any moment.

Desiree made herself focus on the newspaper again. She reread the article then snapped the paper shut.

The familiar tug of guilt that always occurred when she read about her family was starting to surface. Painful memories now threatened to kick in.

The guilt swiftly changed to an agonizing ache. She wasn't the one who had abandoned her family. They'd abandoned her.

Sheer curiosity and a need to belong kept her perusing the paper. She felt compelled to read about the family she was no longer a part of.

Dr. Mason, the admired civil rights leader, still made the news. He'd been around at the same time as Dr. King but their approaches were very different. Whereas Martin Luther King was an advocate of nonviolence, Terry Mason believed in doing whatever it took to make people sit up and listen. The two men had actually been rivals. Dr. Terry had quite a large following but he'd never reached the people the way Dr. King had. That frustrated him greatly and his frustration was vented at home.

Desiree had been a change-of-life baby. Eight years separated her from her sister, the middle child. Desiree was the daughter who'd never fit in, the one who'd struggled through school and rebelled. She'd left home and changed her name. It was not something the Mason family could easily forgive.

It all seemed a lifetime ago and Desiree was now an upstanding citizen, or at least she used to be. Still, she continued to have an insatiable urge to see what the Mason family was up to. Reading about her family was safe. She could fantasize about how life would have been had she remained in Atlanta.

Today's news was not good. The front-page article said her father had been hospitalized. The details, though sketchy, sounded serious.

Desiree's conscience warred with her. For what must

easily be the hundredth time she considered calling Atlanta. But what would be the point? No one from her
family had reached out to her. And who could blame
them? She'd not been in touch in over twenty years. And
she hated her father. Yet the news of his hospitalization
was unnerving.

A jingling phone roused her. She checked caller ID and
picked up. As the rumors about her firing spread, the calls
had increased.

"Zinga," Desiree greeted, "what's up, girl?"

"Just checking to see how you're holding up."

How was she holding up? She was still in shock and
hoping that both Harvey and Byron would call to say that
it was all a figment of her imagination.

"Managing," Desiree said, gloomily. "Trying to make
plans."

"Have you seen the paper today?"

"I'm reading it as we speak."

"Isn't is sad? It's like the end of an era," Zinga wailed,
her voice taking on a husky tone. "We had such hope
back then that we'd overcome."

Zinga had clearly read the article.

"It's not like Dr. Mason is dead," Desiree said, hoping
she didn't sound cold. "And, even if he dies, I'm sure his
spirit will live on."

Zinga moaned. "He might as well be gone. The little
I read doesn't sound good."

There'd been so many times Desiree had wished her fa-

ther dead. Even moments ago she'd gotten a gruesome satisfaction visualizing him confined to a narrow hospital bed.
He was used to being waited on hand and foot by her
mother. Relinquishing control would not come easily to
him.

"Des?" Zinga chirped. "You don't sound yourself. Do
you need me to come over and cheer you up?"

"No, I'm okay."

"I was saying," Zinga continued, still a bit shaken up,
"I'm feeling for Dr. Mason's family. His wife's alive and
I read somewhere he has three children. It's got to be
tough on all of them."

"I'm sure it is."

Zinga didn't have a clue she was Dr. Terry Mason's
daughter, thank God.

What would her friend say if she knew this man she
revered was a wife beater?

There were times at night when Desiree still heard her
mother's anguished screams for help. It was those memories that made Desiree vow never to be a dependant
woman. Her independence had created problems with
Byron.

"Nowhere in the article does it mention Dr. Mason's
condition," Desiree reminded Zinga.

But Zinga seemed certain. "Read between the lines,"
she said. "Dr. Mason must be a hundred years old. If his
hospitalization made news, it's serious."

A slight exaggeration regarding her father's age. But

that damned emotion called guilt was again kicking in. She could so easily pick up the phone and call directory assistance. Desiree's guess was the family still lived in the same sprawling home in that fancy Atlanta suburb.

What would she say? How would she explain two decades of silence and how would she feel talking to the mother she secretly blamed, and didn't respect? How would she justify never answering her mother's initial pleading letters? At one point Ella had actually tracked her down.

Desiree knew hearing her mother's voice would dredge up old memories of that final parting. No, she could not do it. The Masons were no longer part of her life, not her brother Terrence, or her sister Tanya, or her mother herself. She would shelve her concerns in the same manner she'd shelved her mother's desperate efforts to get her to come home. But that was easier said than done. Memories couldn't be stashed in an old hatbox and tossed into the back of a closet. Memories were real. And blood was blood.

But she was worried and feeling guilty. Deep down, she sensed her life was about to undergo another change. And she wasn't sure it would necessarily be for the better.

"I can't do it," she said aloud, "I can't call." The words tumbled out before she could stop them. She'd almost forgotten about Zinga.

"What did you say?" her friend asked. "Des, you're acting mighty peculiar."

"Nothing. It was nice of you to check on me. Now I

have to get back to my chores. Maybe I'll call you later."
But Desiree knew she wouldn't.

The phone rang again

"Desiree?" a male voice inquired, one she couldn't place.

"Yes?" Desiree said carefully. "Who's this?"

"It's Rafiq Jones. How are you doing?"

Desiree whooshed out a breath. She hadn't seen or heard from Rafiq since the night he'd invited her for a drink and Zinga had more or less accused him of sabotage. Desiree had thought his concern for her was genuine though, and he did have the sexiest caramel-colored eyes rimmed by long lashes. She still couldn't understand why he'd been intimidated by Zinga. It seemed somewhat out of character for him.

Should she heed her friend's warning and be wary of Rafiq? Should she question his motives? His interest in her did seem rather sudden. They'd been working at Fannie Jackson for months and he'd never made much of an effort to get to know her until now. Then again, she'd had Byron.

"Rafiq," Desiree said, her tone guarded. "How nice it is to hear from you. I never properly thanked you for taking me out for a drink."

"You did, and quite graciously, too. I'm calling to inquire about your job search. I may have a few leads for you."

She'd left the field wide open for him. Why would he be so magnanimous? Guilt, she decided.

"I haven't even started looking," Desiree admitted.

That much was true. She'd thought about updating her résumé, then shoved it aside. Other things always seemed to take precedence: cleaning out her closet, running, the gym, anything other than looking for a job.

She decided to take charge of the conversation.

"Has Harvey made a decision as to who's stepping into his shoes?" she asked.

"Not that I know of."

He didn't sound too concerned.

Desiree was relentless. "The term ends in a few weeks. He has to announce his replacement soon. Aren't you dying to hear?"

"Whatever the outcome, I'll manage," he said non-committally.

It was a cryptic response and one to be taken out and examined later. Rafiq seemed laid-back about a job that would at least offer him permanency. He didn't seem overly worried, contrary to what she'd been told.

Why should she still care? Her days at Fannie Jackson were over. She was no longer on the faculty. Her energies needed to be focused on finding a new job and soon.

"What about substitute teaching?" Rafiq asked, bringing her back to the here and now. "It would keep you busy and you would get paid."

Why was a virtual stranger so concerned about her well-being? She'd given substitute teaching some thought. It was somewhat of a comedown from where she'd been

but, on the other hand, it would help pay the mortgage—
that is, if anyone would hire a woman with a past.

"I doubt anyone in Bethesda would hire me," Desiree
answered quietly. "Word has gotten out that I was fired.
The rumors are flying and they're ugly."

"Your reputation up until now has got to count for
something."

Why was he being so nice to her?

"On another note," Rafiq said when she didn't answer,
"your father's illness made this morning's paper. It sounds
serious. When will you be going home?"

Desiree couldn't think of a thing to say. How did this
man know Dr. Terry Mason was her father? She used
Alexander, her mother's maiden name. And she'd never
confided in anyone that she and the revered Dr. Mason
were in any way related.

There was no point in denying it. He already knew. But
she was curious.

"How did you know Dr. Mason was my father?" Desiree asked.

Rafiq chuckled. "Oh, I have my ways. "There's another reason I'm calling," he said, switching the subject.
"I'd like to discuss it when you get back?"

"Get back from where?"

"Atlanta."

"I'm not going."

"Yes, you are."

How could he be so certain when even she didn't know?

"You'll want to go home and see your dad and the family. Now that you're no longer working, you should have plenty of time."

Was that a dig or was she being overly sensitive? She would not let Rafiq Jones make her feel guiltier than she already did. Returning to Atlanta was out of the question. Bethesda was now her home.

"Suppose we talk now," Desiree said, her curiosity piqued. "What was the other reason you called?"

"I'd prefer to talk in person. It'll hold until you get back."

He seemed confident that she would go. Desiree had no intention of spending one dime of her limited funds buying a ticket to check on a man that had never been a real father to her.

She was still hanging on to the phone long after the conversation ended. Her thoughts now turned to the big strapping man who called himself her father. Lying in a hospital bed would not be easy for him. He'd hate it. Desiree was still thinking about Dr. Mason when the phone rang again.

"Hello," she answered, her mind elsewhere and forgetting to check her caller ID.

"Hey, girl. Guess where I am?"

The voice sounded vaguely familiar. She couldn't place it. Then it came to her—Sandi.

"Desiree, I'm at Dulles Airport. Can you come get me?" her old roommate whined.

"Who is this?" she asked, needing to know for certain.

"Your best friend, darling, Sandi. I'm here to cheer you up. It will be like old times."

Desiree forced enthusiasm into her voice. "What a nice surprise." Under her breath she groaned, "More like a nightmare."

It was typical of Sandi to assume she could arrive un-expectedly and be welcomed with open arms. Desiree would bet anything Sandi expected her to put her life on hold now that she was here.

"Aren't you eager to see me?" Sandi continued to whine. "Come get me. The cost of a taxi is outrageous. And I don't know where you live."

Desiree rolled her eyes. She was not looking forward to a forty-five minute drive on a rainy highway, nor was she particularly looking forward to having Sandi as her houseguest.

"Maybe you should rent a car," Desiree gently sug-gested, though she already knew there was a fat chance of that happening. "You've always been Ms. Indepen-dent. You'll want to have wheels."

"But I wouldn't know where I was going. I can't read a map. Come get me?" Sandi wheedled like the diva that she was.

Desiree sighed, knowing she would eventually cave. If Sandi was in town she was there for a reason. Last Desiree had heard, Sandi Thomas was a household name in the adult entertainment industry. She made a good living making foreign films and was the toast of Amsterdam.

"Do you have a reservation?" Desiree asked warily as if she didn't already know the answer. "Some place I can drop you off?"

"No. How can you even ask that? I'm staying with you."

Sandi managed to sound horrified. She acted as if Desiree had wounded her deeply. Naturally it left Desiree feeling guilty and ungracious.

Desiree chuckled uneasily. "I just thought I would ask, hon. I never want to assume anything."

"Don't you want me to stay with you?" Sandi asked sharply. "We talked about this when I called before. You invited me."

Like hell she had. Sandi had been the one to suggest coming, but nothing had been agreed to or written in stone. If she thought Sandi would care, Desiree would have told her she was unemployed and had problems of her own.

Taking a deep breath, Desiree debated how best to handle this turn of events. She was reluctant to have Sandi spend any extended time with her, and for a number of reasons. But could she say no and risk the consequences?

Dealing with Sandi on a daily basis would be stressful. She was high maintenance and had a way of getting on peoples' last nerves. Living with Sandi would be like being caught in a hurricane without shelter. On the other hand, if she were willing to pay rent, maybe Desiree could continue with the kitchen renovations she'd put on hold.

"Okay, I'll come and get you," Desiree agreed. "What airline did you fly in on?"

"Delta. I took the shuttle from New York. I'm at the arrivals area."

"Waiting for your bags?" Desiree grimaced at the thought. She figured Sandi was probably traveling movie-star fashion with trunks and garment bags galore. "How long are you planning on staying?"

She held her breath, dreading the answer.

Tinkling laughter followed. "Who knows? Maybe forever."

God help her—perish the thought.

"Okay. I'll be there as soon as I can. Wait on the curb in front of the terminal."

Instead of saying thank-you, Sandi whined, "Why so long? There shouldn't be traffic at this hour."

"I'll be there," Desiree repeated, and hung up.

Almost an hour later, thanks to a steady downpour that snarled up traffic, Desiree pulled up in front of Delta's arrival area. There was no one standing there that looked remotely like Sandi.

Leaving the car illegally parked, Desiree braved the elements and hurried inside. There were a few people hanging around the carousel, but none remotely resembled the friend she remembered. It was pointless getting annoyed.

This was typical of Sandi, who lived in her own little world.

Desiree weaved her way around a bunch of yawning limousine drivers, who were yakking with each other. At the far end of the terminal she spotted Sandi. In typical Sandi fashion she was in deep discussion with a man. He was tall and, from his Burberry coat and rimless glasses, Desiree guessed him to be a businessman. Sandi was the type who went for men with money and large portfolios. From the doting look on this guy's face, he was already smitten.

It was time to make her presence known.

Desiree inserted herself between them. Jingling her keys, she said, "I'm parked illegally, hon. Do you have your luggage?"

"No kiss?" Sandi asked, raising an impeccably polished fingernail and tapping her rouged cheek. Desiree dutifully pecked the spot she pointed to.

"We really have to go before I get a ticket," Desiree insisted, disentangling herself and trying not to breathe in her friend's expensive perfume.

"We will in a minute. Go find my bags while I say goodbye to Glenn."

The nerve. Desiree managed a wintry smile. She was no longer the malleable teenager Sandi remembered.

"I wouldn't recognize your bags, hon," Desiree answered. "You get them and I'll wait in the car. Try not to be too long."

Before Sandi could come back with a fitting retort, Desiree headed off.

It was times like these that Desiree was glad she'd been a schoolteacher. Teaching had given her an abundance of poise. She'd give Sandi exactly ten minutes, then, as far as she was concerned, the actress could rent her own damn car.

If this was any indication of what living with her would be like, advertising for a roommate in the paper was sounding better and better.

Already agitated, Desiree slid behind the wheel of her SUV. No way was she going to let Sandi Thomas run her life. It had happened once. It wouldn't happen again.

CHAPTER 5

"Please have a seat," Harvey Coleman said, waving Rafiq to the chair directly facing him.

Rafiq sat, his eyes roaming the monstrous office, taking in the expensive artwork and numerous sculptures. He refused to let Harvey intimidate him. The dean had requested his presence and it was up to him to initiate the conversation. Rafiq guessed he'd been summoned to discuss the open position. Hopefully, a decision had been made at last.

Harvey sat silently, fiddling with his Mont Blanc pen. He rolled the instrument back and forth between his palms. After several more seconds went by, the dean cleared his throat and lay the pen down on his highly polished desk. He laced his fingers beneath his chin and cleared his throat.

"You'll be pleased with the news," he finally announced.

Rafiq drew in a breath and waited. As much as he wanted this job—no needed it—he would not show Harvey how much getting this appointment meant to him.

"You've made a decision?" Rafiq asked in tones that expressed interest but not desperation.

"Not exactly. The board has not made its decision yet."

Then why was he here?

Harvey's smile now revealed only the bottom half of capped white teeth. He was stalling and obviously waiting for Rafiq to speak. Rafiq decided no comment was the way to go. Harvey was the one who'd summoned him from the faculty lounge. It would be the Harvey Coleman show.

Since Desiree had been removed from the picture, and Phyllis was out sick more often than not, the position should be his. But there were rumors that Phyllis was sleeping with Harvey and that would most certainly give her the edge.

Harvey was now staring at Rafiq over his knuckles. Rafiq met the dean's eyes square on. He wondered what Harvey hoped to achieve by playing these games?

The dean spoke as if to himself. "Rafiq, you are a strong candidate for my position, but there is another person we are also considering. Conrad Maloney is eminently qualified and very well regarded."

Who the hell was Conrad Maloney? And what was

Harvey trying to tell him? How come he hadn't heard the man's name before?

"Who is Conrad Maloney?" Rafiq probed.

Harvey showed another millimeter of teeth. "Conrad is our only outside candidate. He comes to us with excellent credentials and outstanding references."

Was there a hidden message here somewhere? Rafiq also had top-notch references. The people he'd listed were big names and came with sterling reputations. But he wasn't stupid; many a person had lost a job solely because he didn't have the right contacts.

"What will be the deciding factor?" Rafiq asked. "Will there be another interview?"

Harvey's fingers now left the home he'd made for them under his chin. He picked up the Mont Blanc and drummed it against the mahogany desk.

"Our decision will be made after a thorough background check."

"How in-depth of a background check?" Rafiq asked hoping he didn't sound nervous. "Fannie Jackson isn't exactly corporate America. Shouldn't recommendations suffice?"

A background check was not something he had anticipated nor was it something he wanted.

"The board is requiring extensive checks of all the candidates. It's a necessary evil these days." Harvey answered, clearing his throat. "We can't risk having our reputation endangered."

"Of course not," Rafiq repeated. "Of course not." He felt the beads of sweat pop out on his forehead. "The faculty was surprised to see Desiree Alexander leave. She seemed the obvious one to step into your shoes."

Harvey appeared speechless for a moment.

"Yes, Desiree's resignation came as a surprise to all of us." Harvey deigned to show a little more dental work. "We were sorry to see her go."

He rose, signaling the meeting had ended.

Rafiq also stood and shook the dean's hand.

"Thanks for filling me in on what the next steps are. You'll contact me when another interview will be scheduled?"

"Absolutely."

Rafiq was then quickly ushered out.

"You never told me why you and Byron broke up," Sandi probed. She was lying on Desiree's white couch, a couple of pillows propped under her head. She sipped a Cosmopolitan—her third, if Desiree had counted correctly.

"I've told you at least a dozen times that it was just one of those things. We weren't right for each other."

Why the questions? What was it to her?

"What exactly does 'not right for each other' mean?"

Sandi was at it again. Desiree sighed in exasperation. The questions were relentless. Sandi didn't seem to care that she didn't want to talk about Byron. It was a private matter and none of Sandi's business.

"Come on, girlfriend, might as well spill," Sandi persisted.

"Can we change the topic?"

Hopefully that would be the end of that.

What was it with the ongoing drilling? Since she arrived a week ago, Sandi had asked question after question; nothing appeared to be off-limits to her.

Desiree was resenting her presence even more than she'd expected. Maybe it had something to do with feeling that her house and life had been taken over. Sandi had even managed to borrow Desiree's car and get into a minor fender bender, one that she'd insisted she didn't cause, but would cost Desiree plenty. And she hadn't even offered to pay.

It had been one of those freak accidents that wasn't worth reporting to the insurance company. It would cost less than the deductible and would only make her premium go up. Sandi had also managed to break her dishwasher and jam her garbage disposal.

All of these issues, while minor irritations, would cost money to fix. Money Desiree didn't have, and Sandi didn't seem to think was her responsibility to offer. With Desire's credit cards close to the max, and no job on the horizon, these mishaps were disastrous.

Yet, Desiree sucked it up and tried to remain positive. Sandi knew very well she wasn't working. Desiree had been forced to tell her the truth because Sandi had come right out and asked why she was home. Desiree's admission that she'd been fired had elicited peals of laughter followed by a slew of questions. Instead of being compassionate, Sandi saw humor in Desiree's situation.

"I can't believed that old thing's still around!" she'd said. "What's the big deal anyway? Celebrities bare their assets all the time and no one blinks an eye. I say we break out the popcorn and wine, watch the stupid video and have a few laughs."

"It's not funny," Desiree said, thinking it was typical of Sandi to be so cavalier. She'd always been self-involved and at times that translated to being insensitive. Yet, despite these qualities, she could be quite charming and they did have a history of sorts.

Desiree had often thought about why they'd initially bonded. She and Sandi were as unlike as two people could be. Maybe it was the other woman's brassy behavior and general outlook on life that had appealed to her. Sandi didn't seem to give a hoot about what others thought of her. She was high energy, and could be fun when she put her mind to it, and wasn't getting Desiree into trouble.

The liquid in the martini glass Sandi held threatened to slosh. It came close to spilling on Desiree's pristine couch.

"Uh," Desiree said, "do you need to set the glass down? I'll get you a coaster."

Sandi's response was to balance the glass on the armrest, where it teetered precariously. Desiree held her breath. A pink stain would be the devil to get out.

The front doorbell rang. You would have thought Sandi was expecting someone, and maybe she was. She leapt off the couch and raced for the door, putting an eye to the peephole. She turned back. "There's a man out there. You holding out on me?"

"I'm not expecting anyone." Desiree answered, frowning. She wasn't, though her first thought was that it might be Byron whom she hadn't seen or heard from since the time she'd caught him with that woman.

Now it was Desiree's turn to press her eye to the peephole. A pair of broad shoulders and a solid chest filled every inch of lens space. "Who is it?" she asked.

"Rafiq Jones."

Desiree's jaw literally dropped. How did Rafiq know where she lived? And why would he show up without calling? She couldn't pretend she wasn't at home, she'd already answered. She had no choice than to let him in.

"Just a moment."

She took her time unlocking the door.

"Who's Rafiq Jones?" Sandi mouthed.

"Someone I used to work with."

Desiree smoothed her hair and dusted crumbs off her comfortable sweats. There wasn't a heck of a lot she could do about what she looked like now; Rafiq was already here. Opening the door, she faced him.

"This is a surprise."

"I tried calling. I got a busy signal." There was a sober expression on his face. He followed that announcement with a perfunctory kiss on the cheek; a kiss that seemed too intimate given their relationship. "The situation was serious enough to make me take my chances. Luckily I found your address in the teachers' directory." He slapped the newspaper he was carrying into Desiree's hand. "You'd better sit down and read this."

Sandi inserted herself between them. "I'm Sandra Thomas," she said, "Desiree's roommate in from Amsterdam. And who are you?"

Rafiq seemed a bit taken back. He silently assessed Sandi before offering up a terse smile.

"Desiree and I taught together at Fannie Jackson."

Sandi flashed him a coquettish smile. "Maybe I should consider teaching. Who'd guess a high school had teachers as fine as you?"

Rafiq's eyebrow arched, but he deliberately ignored the come-on. "There's been a leak somewhere," he said, turning his attention back to Desiree. "I'm surprised your phone isn't ringing. While you read, Sandi and I can sit in your kitchen and get acquainted. I wouldn't mind having a cup of coffee."

"I'll fix a pot," Sandi said quickly. Taking Rafiq by the hand, she headed off.

When they were out of sight, Desiree unfolded the newspaper with some trepidation. The headline leapt out at her and bile rose in her throat. God, it was worse than she'd thought. Would she ever be able to put this behind her?

Candidate For Dean Porn Queen.

The accompanying article was short and to the point. It supported Fannie Jackson's decision to terminate her employment. She was depicted as a woman with a colorful past who could corrupt young children and should never have been hired.

Chastising herself again for her stupidity, Desiree snapped the paper shut. Just when she'd thought things were settling down, something like this had to happen. She didn't have a prayer in the world of ever finding a job in Bethesda now.

The skewered account of her fall from grace only made her angrier. It was clear that someone had it in for her. And she meant to find out who. Zinga's warning rang in her ear; she'd said Rafiq Jones was no friend. If that was the case, why had he made a point to come find her? Was he intentionally rubbing it in her face?

Where were her so-called friends anyway? Her phone hadn't exactly been ringing off the hook with offers of support. Those who called were looking for gossip. Even Conrad Maloney, the assistant principal at a nearby school and someone she considered a good friend, had fallen off the face of the earth.

She'd been out of work exactly two weeks. She and Conrad used to make a point of having lunch whenever they could. They'd trade gossip about their respective schools. If one or the other couldn't meet, it was customary for them to call.

"Desiree," Sandi said, returning to the living room

with a steaming cup in her hand, "how about a cup of coffee?" Rafiq was nowhere to be seen.

After thanking her, Desiree accepted the cup and set it down. Sandi stayed, surprising her by flopping down next to her. "Is everything okay?" she asked. "What was that article about? Can I see it?"

There was no point in hiding the evidence from Sandi. It was public knowledge. The newspaper had probably been read by hundreds if not thousands of people; all of whom had formed an opinion of her. Desiree handed the newspaper over and turned away.

Sandi shook out the wrinkles before carefully perusing the paper. Several times she laughed out loud.

"Well, girlfriend," she said, setting the paper aside, "if nothing else, you won't be forgotten soon."

"I don't want to be remembered because of a scandal," Desiree cried. "I worked my butt off to get where I am. It cost me plenty to earn my degrees."

"Aren't you a couple of credits short of a PhD?"

Desiree shrugged. "It doesn't much matter now. I'll be lucky to get hired as a waitress in this town."

Sandi, remembering she'd abandoned Rafiq, slid off the couch and handed Desiree back the paper. "I better go see to our guest," she said. "What's his story? Is he single? Straight?"

Some things never changed. Although she felt like crap, her sense humor kicked in. "You're incorrigible. I never thought to ask."

"Why not?"

"Because the man's availability doesn't interest me."

"It interests me," Sandi said without missing a beat.

"Then don't waste time talking to me. Ask him yourself."

"Ask me what?" Rafiq said, coming up behind them.

Sandi had the grace to look embarrassed. It was the first time Desiree had seen her visibly flustered.

"It's girl talk," Desiree answered, covering for her friend.

"How are you feeling?" Rafiq asked Desiree. "That was quite the article."

"Yes, it was. It made me sound so dirty."

"Must have been a slow day in the newsroom."

Bless him for attempting to keep things light.

The phone rang just then. Desiree froze.

"Let the answering machine pick up," Rafiq suggested. But Sandi had already headed off to answer.

"Check caller ID if you have it," Rafiq shouted after her. "You might want to screen your calls and I'd suggest you not answer the door without checking first."

She supposed he was right. Reporters would be trying to reach her and so would curiosity seekers. She'd been depicted as the ex-porn queen. Her dismissal would make for a good human interest story, a fallen woman masquerading as an instructor at a prestigious private school.

CHAPTER 6

Ella Mason paced the sprawling Victorian home that she privately referred to as her prison. For forty-something of the fifty years she'd been married, she'd felt as if she'd been serving a sentence.

Most people wished they had her life. She had little to complain about, or so they thought. Ella lived large. She had all the trappings of success. She had the big house and the luxury sedan, the housekeeper and the prominent husband. Ella had it all.

Her friends envied her. Terrence Mason had been quite the catch. He'd bought her all the material things she could hope for and then some. Why then did she feel empty and as if she were living a lie?

She *was* living a lie. Her grown children knew it, too,

because they'd escaped as soon as they could. Her youngest hadn't even waited to come of age. Her baby had run off and found a man old enough to be her father. When he'd grown tired of her, he'd moved on. But Desiree, stubborn child that she was, hadn't returned home. She'd turned her back on Atlanta and the family that had raised her. It seemed a lifetime had gone by without a word. Desiree's wish to sever family ties had broken Ella's heart.

There were times Ella thought she no longer had a heart to break. In its place was a void. She'd endured her husband's philandering with a stoic face, and that effort had wrung the last bit of emotion out of her. Now numbness had taken emotion's place.

What would possess a child she'd raised—one who'd been given everything she needed—to cut family ties and run away from home?

Ella relied on Tanya, her oldest, the one who'd married Terrence Senior's godson, for news of Desiree. It was through her she'd learned that Desiree had settled down and gone into teaching. Tanya had even gone on the Internet and tracked down Desiree's address. Ella knew she lived in Maryland.

Ella glanced at her Cartier watch, the one Terrence had given her as a fiftieth anniversary present. Terry Junior, who'd promised to pick her up, was late. He should have been here twenty minutes ago to drive her to the hospital, as he'd done every day since his father had the stroke.

That child was an enigma to her. He was equally as

closemouthed as his father was verbose. At forty-six years old, he should have been married, but Ella had never even seem him with a woman. All he talked about was work, work, work.

A horn honked in the driveway and Ella glanced out the picture window. Terry was seated in his silver BMW, one ear pressed to his cell phone. She'd not brought him up to be so disrespectful. Had his father been home, he would not have put up with the honking. That child would have been forced to get out and come in to fetch her.

Terry always acted as if he hated the house he'd grown up in. He even acted as if he hated her. But, though the boy kept his distance, his father worshiped the ground his lawyer son walked on.

Sighing, Ella gathered her purse. She called to Winnetta, who'd been her housekeeper for almost as many years as Ella had been married. Winnetta was more like family than an employee. And she took care of Ella in ways her husband couldn't. She provided emotional support.

"I'm leaving," Ella shouted. "I'll be back soon as I can."

Winnetta emerged from the kitchen, where she'd been preparing dinner. She looked worried. She wiped her hands on her apron and said, "Take your time, Mrs. Mason, I'll be here holding down the fort. I'm praying, Lord, you know I'm praying. Dr. Mason just gotta get better. Don't seem fair that he was struck down. You make sure to tell him I'm thinking of him."

The blast of the horn came from out front. Winnetta rolled her eyes. "What's wrong with that boy? Why is he so impatient? He should take his big strapping self out of that fancy car and walk up the driveway. He has better manners than that."

Ella figured maybe it was time to go before Winnetta really got on a roll. She wouldn't put it past her feisty housekeeper to step outside, grab her son by the ear and give him what for.

"I'll try to be back for dinner," Ella added. "If I'm not just leave everything in the oven and I'll warm it up."

"Don't seem right you should be eating by yourself when you have two grown children."

"Three," Ella automatically answered.

Winnetta sucked her teeth. "That girl might as well be dead. We don't hear nothing from her. Far as I'm concerned she doesn't exist."

It was definitely time to leave. Another earsplitting honk confirmed it.

Winnetta, although she had to be in her late seventies, beat Ella to the front door. She yanked open the heavy wooden doors and stuck her head out. "Your mother's coming, boy. The whole neighborhood don't need to know how disrespectful you are."

Ella pushed past Winnetta and headed out. Her son was courteous enough to end his cell phone call. Unfolding his long limbs, he got out to hold the passenger door open.

"Hello, Mother," Terry greeted her. "You've kept me waiting long enough. I don't know how you put up with that witch," he said, referring to Winnetta. "She needs to be taken down a peg or two."

"Winnetta is not a witch," Ella said smoothly. "She has always been like a second mother to you. You should have come inside to get me."

Ella actually felt good saying what she thought. It was seldom she got to express her true opinion.

Terry Junior gestured to the backseat of the car where he'd stashed his briefcase and at least half a dozen manila folders. "Can we get going? I've got briefs to go over. Tomorrow I go to court."

"Well, I didn't exactly hold you up," Ella pointed out. "You were on the phone taking care of your business."

Terrence ignored her and turned the key in the ignition. "Let's just hope there's no traffic."

He was so uptight. She'd never seen him dressed in anything other than a tie and jacket. She chose to ignore Winnetta's snide comments about her son being a closet homosexual. There was no love lost between the two and Winnetta used every waking minute to drive that point home.

The fifteen-minute drive to the hospital passed in almost total silence. Ella's attempts to draw her son out produced one-word answers. She should be used to that. For some inexplicable reason, people said Terry looked just like Bryant Gumble, but that was pretty much where the similarities ended. His communication skills were sorely lacking.

At last Terrence pulled the car up in front of the hospital. Ella looked at him questioningly. "Aren't you coming in?"

"No. I'll be back for you when you're ready. You have my cell number, Mother."

Ella contemplated how best to handle him. She hated conflict of any kind, but something needed to be said.

"You haven't visited your father since the night he was brought into the hospital," she reminded Terry. "Don't you think he will wonder why?"

Terry shrugged. "I don't visit him when he's well. Why should anything change?"

"Because he's your father, Terrence, that's why. He raised you."

"He's your husband. And he did not raise me. You and that pushy housekeeper did. The man lived in our house and paid for things. And at night he abused you."

He knew. Her son knew, though he had never articulated it before. Did Tanya know, too? And did Desiree know? Was that why her baby had taken off? Her youngest was still her baby and would always be. She missed her, God did she miss her. Ella had done everything possible to shield her children from the ugly truth and to preserve her husband's image.

Terrence Senior was considered a pillar of Atlanta society. He was well respected by people of every age. Most remembered him as the young activist, always giving Martin Luther King a run for his money and encouraging their people to gather arms and fight for what they believed in. The elders still recounted his civil rights efforts and his battle for equality.

They would never believe that Dr. Mason was a wife beater. It was something even Ella denied. Terrence only hit her when she butted heads with him. It was her fault he was hospitalized. She was responsible for his stroke. They'd had a fight and she'd said terrible things. If she'd kept her mouth shut he would not be in the hospital fighting for his life.

A rap on the passenger window made Ella jump. She looked up to see Tanya motioning to her to open the window.

Terrence Junior pushed a button on the center console. He nodded at his sister, but didn't say a word.

"What took you so long to get here, Mama?" Tanya demanded, ignoring her brother. "I've got a husband and kids to feed. I need to get home."

"What happened to 'Hello, mother'?" Ella asked, the door already half-open. "How is your father, anyway?"

"Asking for you. The doctor thinks he might have had another mild stroke."

One of Ella's hands patted her heart. "Oh, my Lord! Why didn't someone call me?"

"Because nobody knew until the doctor checked on

him. Come on, Mother, I'll walk you up, then I really have to go."

"Did you hear that?" Ella said, turning back to her son. "Your dad might have had another minor stroke."

Terrence Junior shrugged. "He's not dead, Mother. Depending who you ask, that's not a bad thing."

"How could I have given birth to someone so heartless?"

Tanya, who stood witnessing the entire exchange, tapped her foot impatiently. "Mother, please don't waste your breath on Terry. Dad's waiting and I need to take off."

The moment Ella closed the car door, Terrence sped away.

Ella huffed out a breath. "I don't understand that child. He's cold and uncaring. He never used to be like this."

"Believe what you want to believe. Terrence has always been like that. He's got his reasons, I suppose."

On the elevator, Ella questioned Tanya about her father's condition.

"Dr. Spence doesn't seem to be overly worried. He says it's not uncommon for stroke victims to have several mild attacks."

"Did it affect his speech further?" Ella asked.

"It's still slurred and the right side of his face is even more twisted."

The elevator arrived on the eighth floor and they got off. Ella could barely keep up with Tanya's long strides.

"Have you tried reaching Desiree?" Ella asked as they approached the room.

"No, Mother. I did not. Dad's illness made national news. If Desiree wanted to know how he was, she would have called by now."

Ella didn't want to believe her youngest daughter would be that callous. "What if she doesn't remember the phone number?"

Tanya sighed exasperatedly. "You haven't moved, Mother. You've lived in the same home for over forty years. Today there are lots of different ways of getting someone's number. If Desiree wanted to find you, she could."

They entered the private room. Any mention of Desiree was strictly off-limits now. As far as Terry was concerned, she no longer existed. She was the wild child who'd bucked the system and gone astray.

"I'll say goodbye to dad, then I'm taking off," Tanya reminded Ella.

True to her word, she approached the sick bed and gave her father's forehead a quick kiss. Terrence appeared to be asleep. Tanya turned and gave Ella a hug before ducking out of the room.

Ella took a seat in a chair at the foot of the bed. She looked at her husband, who seemed to have shrunk in size. His breathing was shallow and even in repose the right side of his face was distorted. She thought about all the years they had spent together. She'd married him at twenty and he was all that she knew. What would she do if the good Lord saw fit to take him from her? How would she cope?

A nurse entered, one of many who came and went.

"Did you get any rest, Mrs. Mason?" she asked. "You'll need to keep up your strength."

Ella nodded. The nurse didn't need to know that her rest consisted of fitful catnaps. Ella hadn't gotten a good night's sleep since Winnetta found Terry facedown on the library floor. She'd been sick with worry wondering how she would cope if anything happened to him.

She was luckier than most, at least she had a college degree. That was practically unheard of for a woman of her era, and an even bigger accomplishment for a black female. Though a lot of good that would do her at her age. No one would ever hire her. She'd never made an important decision in her life. Terry had always taken charge. No, she couldn't imagine what life would be like should Terry die.

He would get better, Ella vowed. Life had not always been easy with him. But none of her friends' lives were easy. If it wasn't one thing it was another. You weighed the bad against the good. In the whole scheme of things, life with Terry wasn't awful. She just had to make sure she didn't upset him. Ella had gotten very good at defusing tense situations over the years. After all, she'd had the children to consider.

A gurgling sound came from Terry's bed. His mouth worked, but no words came out. Ella was at his side in a flash. Terry's eyes were closed but his body jerked rhythmically. He looked as if he were reacting to an electrical prod. A trail of spittle came from the side of his mouth.

Ella panicked. "Nurse," she screamed. "I need a nurse, a doctor, somebody!"

Her own breath came in little gasps. She was hyperventilating and couldn't seem to stop. She was vaguely aware of someone entering the room and of gentle hands easing her back to the chair she'd vacated.

"Put your head between your knees and breathe, honey," a female voice ordered.

Ella had sense enough to realize there was a commotion around Terry's bed. She needed to get to him and see what was going on. She tried to get up but those same hands kept her firmly imprisoned in the chair.

"There's nothing you can do until we get him stabilized," the nurse said.

Ella managed to formulate a question. "Is he having another stroke? I need to know what's going on."

"You'll get a full report as soon as your husband is resting and comfortable. Why don't you go to the cafeteria and get a cup of coffee."

"I can't leave. What if…"

"We'll page you if we need you." This time she was helped out of the chair and steered toward the door.

Ella gave a parting look at the bed. Terry was surrounded by a team of people and totally shielded from her view.

Reluctantly she left, her mind filled with the frightening thought: What if this was the last time she saw her husband alive?

CHAPTER 7

The moment the news broke, Desiree's phone rang off the hook. She heard from people she hadn't heard from in years. Finally she simply stopped answering. Reporters were camped on her doorstep or calling from newspapers she didn't even know existed. She was forced to scan the surrounding area when she came and went. She'd even resorted to wearing an old baseball cap and sunglasses when she went out.

Sandi, of course, loved the drama. She kept a vigilant eye on the caller ID, announcing the parties with barely concealed excitement. And, whenever she could, she questioned Desiree about Rafiq Jones.

Since Desiree didn't know the man well there wasn't much to tell. Desiree only admitted that at the beginning of the school term he was introduced as the visiting history teacher.

"I'm still dying to find out if he's available." Sandi pouted.

"How would I know? You should have asked all those questions the other night."

"I wonder if he's seeing anyone."

Desiree shrugged. "I've never seen him with a woman, if that's what you're asking. So I have to presume there's no Mrs. Jones in the picture."

Sandi seemed reasonably satisfied with that explanation. "Well, he's not wearing a gold band, which means he's up for the taking."

Desiree rolled her eyes. Sandi was obviously interested in Rafiq Jones.

When the phone rang again, Sandi raced toward it. "It's Byron Fisher," she announced gleefully. "I wonder if he's had second thoughts?"

"I don't want to speak to him. Let the machine pick up."

"Come on," Sandi urged. "Satisfy my curiosity. See what he wants."

She lifted the receiver and spoke into it. "For you," she said, handing over the receiver.

Desiree muttered something under her breath. "Yes?" she said, trying to keep her voice even.

"Who answered the phone?" Byron asked.

"A friend."

"Is she staying with you?"

"Yes." Desiree gave Sandi a pointed look, wishing she would disappear.

"What's this garbage I've been reading in the paper? How come you didn't let me know you'd been fired?"

"I have no obligation to you," Desiree countered. "Why would you care?"

"I do care, very much," Byron answered, lowering his voice an octave until it was soft and seductive. "I've loved you for a very long time."

Desiree let a beat or two go by. Weeks had gone by without a word from Byron. What did he want now? She was suddenly furious.

"You have a damn funny way of showing it," she finally said.

"It was that damn career of yours that broke us up. You spent more time with the children you taught than with me."

"Baloney. You wanted out, Byron. You already had another woman lined up." Desiree was conscious of Sandi shamelessly listening. "Now, what is it I can do for you?"

She had expected old memories to surface, but speaking with him just made her mad. This was a man she'd been intimate with, but he'd betrayed her trust. Once trust was lost there was no getting it back. Even if they managed to patch things up it would never be the same. And there was the matter of that other woman.

"I was worried about you and concerned," Byron said,

trying to placate her. "I've regretted how things ended and I'd like to come by and make amends."

"That's not possible."

"And why is that?"

She didn't owe him an explanation, but she gave him one anyway.

"I don't want to see you, Byron."

Desiree caught Sandi's eye. The actress's eyebrows were at ceiling level. "Let him come over," she mouthed. "Don't be too hasty."

The truth of the matter was that Desiree had nothing left to say to Byron Fisher. Seeing him would be pointless. Besides, she suspected that his relationship might have ended and she was the backup. She would be damned if she would make herself convenient for any man.

"Come on, don't be like that," Byron cajoled.

A click on the line signaled a call coming in. Desiree couldn't think of a more timely sound.

"I have to go," she said, depressing the flash button and cutting Byron off. Even the barrage of questions tossed at her from a nosey reporter sounded good right now—any other voice than Byron's.

"Hello," Desiree said the moment the other party came on the line.

"Desiree?" a female voice asked tentatively.

"She's not available. Who is this?"

A pause followed before the person said, "This is her sister, Tanya. Do you know when she'll be back?"

Desiree felt herself tense up. Something terrible must have happened. She remained tongue-tied. Tanya, the sister she hadn't spoken to in years, was on the line, and Desiree had become that resentful little girl again. She braced herself for what was to come.

"Are you still there?" Tanya queried, sounding a little agitated.

"I can take a message," Desiree finally said.

"Whom am I speaking with?"

Desiree didn't want to lie outright. But her past was slowly closing in. She'd just dealt with one unpleasant call; she just couldn't handle another. Conscious of Sandi hovering, she repeated, "I said I'd take a message."

"My number is…" Tanya then proceeded to rattle off her phone number while Desiree scribbled. "Be sure to tell her that it's extremely urgent that she call. Our mother wants to speak with her."

Not her mother, Ella, the one person she'd been close too and loved more than life itself.

"I'll be sure to do that," Desiree said, quickly disconnecting.

Still conscious of Sandi's eyes on her, Desiree sank into a nearby chair.

"You need a glass of wine," Sandi said, disappearing into the kitchen.

Desiree was left with a million thoughts mulling around her head. Tanya had been the older sister, the responsible one, and Desiree had adored her. She'd loved trying on her makeup and clothing. She'd gone to her for advice, advice that was freely given. Tanya had encouraged her to be brave enough to live her own life.

Yet, during all these years, Tanya had never once reached out to her, until today. Conversely, Desiree hadn't reached out to her family, either. She now had to decide whether she wanted to return the call or not. Any contact with any Mason would be like opening up Pandora's box. Desiree wasn't sure she wanted to go there.

What did she say to the family she'd been estranged from? What excuse could she possibly make for her intentional silence? How could she expect her family to understand that for her own self-preservation she'd needed to cut all ties?

Sandi reappeared, bringing a bottle of wine and two glasses with her. She poured the wine and waited for Desiree to take the first sip.

"What did Tanya want?" she asked at last.

"I don't know."

"Will you call her back?"

"I don't know that either."

"You must be curious," Sandi persisted. "My guess is that it has something to do with your father. I know you've been estranged, but Tanya did initiate that call."

"Yes, I suppose that counts for something."

Sandi set her glass down and looked Desiree in the eye. "You won't be able to live with yourself if you don't return that call. You need to find out what Tanya wants."

Sandi knew her too well. She'd also read that newspaper and knew her father was ill. They'd even talked about it briefly.

"I'm not ready to reconnect yet," Desiree answered, "I need a day or so to collect my thoughts and figure out how to proceed."

It was a huge admission on Desiree's part, but true nevertheless.

"Don't put it off too long," Sandi admonished, "or it might be too late. You don't do guilt well—you'll regret it."

Desiree had thought about that. She'd thought about how she would feel if she opened the paper and read that her father had passed away. Yet making the connection again was bound to open up wounds that had never fully healed, even after all these years.

She remembered the distant man who'd rebuffed her efforts to hug him as a child. Sometimes at night she could still hear her mother's muffled cries as the crack of an open hand connected with flesh. And she heard the demeaning taunts.

Desiree was still wrapped up in the awful memories when the front door buzzer rang.

Sandi was already up and heading to see who it might be. She placed an index finger to her lips while pressing an eye to the peephole. Turning back she said, "There's a hot-looking guy outside. Could this be your Byron?"

"Hot is not a word I would use for that man." Desiree didn't even try to hide her bitterness. "It better not be him."

Sandi moved aside and Desiree slid into the spot where she'd been standing. "Yes, it's him all right. What balls!"

Impatient, Byron depressed the buzzer again.

"We can't just ignore him," Sandi whispered. "Your car's out front."

Desiree shook her head. "So what if he did see my car? He has no right to pop over here without calling." She paused, blowing out an exasperated breath. "Okay, might as well get it over with. I'll make it clear to him there isn't a snowball's chance in hell of our having a reconciliation."

"Sure you want to do that? Think about it a little. It's difficult finding a brother making the kind of money Byron does. He's come back to you and that should count for something."

"Hmmph! I don't want another woman's leftovers. I don't give a crap how much he makes," Desiree hissed, reaching for the doorknob. "I'll try to get rid of him as quickly as I can."

The moment the door opened, Byron breezed in. He acted as if he didn't have a care in the world. The expensive trench coat he wore flapped wide open revealing a shirt with a monogram. He was the type of man who took women's breath away. Sandi clearly thought so, too. She let out an audible gasp, her expression indicating she liked what she saw.

Byron reached out to envelop Desiree in his arms. She stepped back, placing distance between them. "I was on my way out," she said breathlessly.

After nodding in Sandi's direction, Byron murmured, "Can we have a few minutes alone?"

Desiree quickly made introductions then said, "I can give you five minutes, then I'm afraid I have to leave."

Sandi, meanwhile, had graciously disappeared somewhere, but Desiree knew she would be listening to every word of the exchange.

"What is it you wanted?" Desiree asked, still leaving him standing.

"I want to talk. Breaking up with you is a mistake I still regret."

"It's too late, Byron," Desiree said, pacing. "I've already moved on."

"What! You found yourself another man?"

He sounded as if that was an impossibility. Desiree stopped her pacing and stared at him.

"If you haven't, there shouldn't be a problem," Byron challenged.

The nerve of the man. His expectation was that he could waltz right back in and pick up where he left off. Wrong! She would have none of that.

"The problem," Desiree said, after more seconds stretched out, "is that you destroyed my faith in you. I would never be able to trust you again. That doesn't make for a good relationship."

"So you're willing to turn your back on all the good years we had?" Byron looked at her as if she'd lost her mind.

"I'm willing to chalk them up as lessons we learn in life."

Byron harrumphed. "You'd be willing to walk away from something special?"

"Whoa! Hold on a minute. You apparently didn't think our time was special. You were the one who stepped out on me. It makes me wonder if you're back because you got dumped."

At that point, Byron threw his hands in the air as if he were surrendering. "I give up!" he shouted. "I came to you willing to let bygones be bygones. You won't give me an inch."

"Why should I?"

"Because you're a woman of a certain age. You no longer have a job and you're unmarried. There's no one to help you out financially. Most women would be gnawing at the bit just thinking of what I'm offering."

"And what are you offering? To me you are used goods."

Byron had finally pushed every hot button there was to push. Desiree seldom got loud but this time she was sure the neighboring condos could hear them. She didn't care.

Byron was actually speechless. He towered above her glowering.

"Support isn't something you've ever been good at," Desiree continued. "And sexual relief, well, I can get that with a battery-operated device. It wouldn't have to be given directions, either."

Byron's honey-colored skin was streaked with crimson.

Desiree could tell from his heightened color that attacking his male prowess might not have been a good idea. He was one fuse short of an explosion.

"I see I've wasted my time," he said, drawing himself up and belting his coat in the process. "I was actually here to offer my services and encourage you to sue the pants off that newspaper for defiling your character. I was going to offer you my contacts to secure you a job. Now I can see coming over here was a waste of time. I'm sorry to have bothered you."

Desiree's response was to hold the door open. Byron, gathering his last shred of dignity, sailed through. The moment the door shut behind him, Sandi popped out of where she'd been hiding.

"Well, you certainly told him off," she said laughing. "Why didn't you just keep him dangling?"

"Because he's not what I want."

Sandi flopped onto the couch, her favorite position. "And what is it you want? There aren't that many options out there for a woman pushing forty." She echoed Byron's words.

"So everyone keeps telling me. My top priority has to be to find a job. Until that's accomplished I don't have the time or energy to think about anything else."

"All right," Sandi said, still looking amused. "What are you going to do about finding a job?"

"I'm going to think long and hard about putting this place up for sale and moving. That's what I'm going to do."

Sandi came to a full upright position. "And where will you move to? Real estate has gotten awfully expensive."

Why was it that everyone felt it necessary to point out the obvious?

"You think I don't know that?" Desiree asked, allowing a faint smile to curl her lips. "I'll just have to figure something out. What about you? How long are you planning on staying in the States?"

Sandi shrugged. "Who knows? I might decide to never go back. It's time for me to settle down. I've been out of the country far too long."

Desiree hoped Sandi wasn't planning on staying here with her. While at times it might be nice to have company, she'd grown used to being on her own.

"What about your career? You're a household name in Europe," Desiree asked carefully. "Starting over here is going to be difficult."

Sandi didn't seem that concerned. Another shrug followed. "I've got a few strings I can pull," she answered. "There are European directors I've worked with before who are now living in California. They know my reputation."

"So you would get back into the X-rated market here?"

"If I had to."

So Sandi might be moving on shortly. Desiree silently thanked the Lord.

"Then again," Sandi said, "since I like it here so much, I might just commute. This would be a good home base.

I've also been thinking it's time for me to get a social life and I know just where I might start."

This time Desiree's smile was one of amusement. "Let me guess. With the man you met at the airport?"

"Wrong!"

Sandi's answering smile reminded Desiree of the cat who'd been caught with her paw in the milk pitcher.

"Nah, I was thinking of Rafiq Jones. I've made no bones about telling you he's fine. And boyfriend sure as heck looks virile. Something tells me I could do worse."

Desiree simply stared at her. Not a word would come out.

CHAPTER 8

Rafiq removed his glasses and set them down on the desk. He stared at the blank computer screen, willing the mental block away. He just couldn't seem to commit one word to paper. Two hours had raced by and he was still unable to formulate a coherent sentence.

It wasn't as if thoughts weren't milling around his head. But how to express them? He'd sworn to tell the truth no matter how difficult that truth was. He'd made a pact with God to share his experiences if another parent could be spared.

It was one thing to make a pact and another to actually go through the process of baring his soul. Strangers would have access to some very private family moments.

But writing, which was supposed to be cathartic, would assuage his guilt.

The signs had been there loud and clear. Yet he and Liz had chosen to ignore them. They knew their son had problems, but blamed his behavior on growing pains.

If they'd acted earlier, could John's death have been avoided? There'd been telltale signs of a child severely depressed, but he and Liz had refused to believe that John was not taking his medication. Guilt still riddled Rafiq. And the nightmares still came, surfacing at the most inopportune moments. He'd see himself coming home, opening up that garage door and finding John swinging from the ceiling.

Focus, Rafiq. Leave it alone. What little spare time there is, you need to dedicate to your book.

Writing helped fill his evenings, the long empty nights when gardening was no longer an option. It helped soothe his soul.

What he really needed was someone to organize his notes, someone with time to spare. Maybe Desiree would consider helping him. It would keep her busy and he would offer to pay. He sensed she could be trusted and would handle the confidences he shared with dignity. Plus they had something in common. They'd both fallen from grace and had to start over.

Rafiq picked up the phone and punched in Desiree's programmed number. She might have gone home to Atlanta; if so, he'd leave a message. The phone rang and the machine picked up. Desiree's sultry voice repeated her number.

"You've reached Desiree. I'm not available. Leave your name and number and I'll call you back."

"This is Rafiq," he said, before he changed his mind. "Call me when you're back and let's talk about the project I mentioned."

He was about to leave his number when a woman's voice came on the line. "Wait. Don't hang up."

It didn't sound like Desiree. It must be the friend.

"Is Desiree there?" Rafiq asked.

"No, she stepped out but you're welcome to come over and have dinner with us. I'm sure she'd like that. I'd like that, too."

He was starving. The invitation came at a good time, since he hadn't given the first thought to dinner. It would be good to be among people. He'd isolated himself for far too long.

"I'd love to join you," Rafiq quickly answered, "providing Desiree wouldn't mind."

"I told you she'd love it. The other teachers have pretty much abandoned her except for that awful Zinga woman."

Rafiq found himself excited at the prospect of having dinner with Desiree. It had been a long time since any woman had held his interest. He'd had a storybook romance with his ex-wife, Liz, whom he'd married right out of college. Two years, and what must have been a dozen fertility treatments, later, they'd had John. Rafik had been on top of the world.

But his delight quickly changed to dismay. The love of

his life, and his best friend, didn't have time for him after that child was born. All Liz talked about was the baby she toted around. A baby that had been difficult from the onset; sweet as could be at one moment, then given to disruptive tantrums and crying spells that could go on for days.

Finally, at age twelve, John was diagnosed as having bipolar disorder. He was prescribed Lithium to control his erratic mood swings. Though the marriage was already in trouble, Rafiq was willing to hang in there. His vows were for better or worse. And his son needed him even if his wife didn't care.

Determined to put painful memories behind him, he hurriedly got dressed.

"What do you mean you invited Rafiq Jones for dinner?" Desiree asked, facing Sandi in the kitchen. "And what exactly are you planning to feed him? I haven't been shopping in days."

"Oh, come on, Desiree, between the two of us we should be able to whip something up. Check the kitchen cabinets—there's got to be something stashed."

Desiree had just returned from meeting with a recruiter. He'd told her what she already knew: her only chances for employment were in another state, and even then her background could easily be checked and any newspaper articles about her read. Feeling frustrated and vilified, she was still debating what to do about Tanya's call.

"Rafiq called asking for you. He wants to discuss

some project. He's quite the catch. If you're not interested, I am."

Despite her irritation, Desiree's curiosity was piqued. Having large portions of unstructured time was beginning to take its toll. It just might be interesting to find out what Rafiq had in mind.

"I suppose we could put together a salad and pasta dish if we had to. I've got shrimp in the freezer," she said, liking the idea of having company more and more. If nothing else Rafiq would be a buffer between her and Sandi.

"I picked up a couple of bottles of wine the other day," Sandi said. "The white's in the refrigerator chilling."

"I don't think Rafiq drinks," Desiree said, remembering the time at the restaurant.

"That's surprising. I wonder if that indicates a drinking problem?"

Trust Sandi to think of something like that. But it did make Desiree think. In so many ways Sandi was far more worldly than she.

"If that's the case, at least he's smart enough to recognize it's a problem," Desiree answered. "What I'm trying to figure out is why he has suddenly taken an interest in me."

"Maybe it's me he's interested in," Sandi said, tossing back her full head of weaved hair. "Maybe I'm the excuse why he keeps coming back."

Modesty had never been one of Sandi's virtues.

"Could be," Desiree said diplomatically, though Rafiq had never shown any sign of interest in her friend.

Desiree again remembered Zinga's warning not to trust Rafiq. She admitted it was peculiar he'd barely given her the time of day when they worked together, and now he suddenly wanted to be friends.

"Come on, you must have the goods on him," Sandi joked. "A man like him with a decent job usually has his pick of women."

"Sorry, can't help you there. I've told you before, I know very little about the man. We'd better get to work or he'll be here before you know it."

They'd just finished making a salad and Desiree was busy sautéing the shrimp when the buzzer rang.

"Do I look okay?" Sandi asked, straightening the pencil-thin skirt she'd slipped into only moments ago and fluffing her voluminous weave.

"You look fine. But you always do. You know that."

Sandi quickly reapplied her lipstick, then hurried off to get the door. Desiree remained in the kitchen to lower the heat under the scampi and put on a pot of water for the pasta.

She heard a low male voice greet Sandi and Sandi's rather effusive greeting.

"Rafiq, so good to see you. Let me take your jacket."

"Where's Desiree?" Rafiq asked.

"Desiree," Sandi called. "Rafiq's here."

Desiree was left with little choice but to leave the safety

of the kitchen and go out to welcome Rafiq. She found Sandi fussing over him, making a production of taking his tweed jacket and the cap he wore.

On seeing Desiree, Rafiq quickly extricated himself from Sandi's hold on his arm and came over to give Desiree a perfunctory kiss on the cheek.

"I hope I'm not imposing," he said, a teasing twinkle in his eye. "You look wonderful. Getting out of academia has done you good."

"What about me? Don't I look wonderful, too?" the irrepressible Sandi interjected.

"You are an absolute vision," Rafiq added gallantly.

"Can we offer you something to drink?" Desiree asked, trying to cover up the fact that his compliment totally flustered her.

"I'll take water if you have it."

Sandi flashed her a look, which Desiree chose to ignore. She hurried back into the kitchen to get Rafiq bottled water and returned with a tray holding water, the bottle of wine and two glasses.

Rafiq was now seated on the couch and Sandi was curled up as close to him as it was humanly possible. Desiree set down the tray on the coffee table and took a seat on the other side of Rafiq.

"Dinner should be ready shortly," she said once they were settled and Rafiq was sipping on his water. "Now, what's this proposal I might be interested in?"

"Let's talk after dinner," Rafiq said, slanting Sandi a

look. He sniffed appreciatively. "Something sure smells good."

"That's my shrimp scampi," Sandi said, taking all the credit for a dish she'd had little input in.

Desiree wanted to strangle her, but managed a gracious smile.

"I can't wait to sample. You ladies really shouldn't have gone to all of this trouble, especially for someone you really weren't expecting."

"No trouble at all." This came from Sandi.

Rafiq then chose to switch the topic of conversation. "Desiree, who's Conrad Maloney?"

The question took her by surprise. "Conrad is a friend of mine, at least he used to be. I haven't heard from him in some time—not since my dismissal."

"That would figure."

A knot settled in Desiree's throat, one she tried to ignore.

"What can I tell you about Conrad?" she asked.

"Anything you care to."

"He's with one of the local private schools. He's an assistant principal."

"Extremely well respected, I've been told, and a candidate for Harvey Coleman's position."

"What?" She couldn't mask her surprise. That explained Conrad's silence.

"Didn't you say this guy was a friend of yours?" Rafiq probed while Sandi listened shamelessly. "You'd have to wonder why he never mentioned he was in the running for Harvey's position."

Rafiq was saying exactly what she was thinking.

"Can't we talk about something other than shop?" Sandi whined, probably irritated that the attention was not on her. "Desiree lost her job, so why would she care if some guy chose not to mention he'd applied for the same position as she?"

Desiree shot her a look. Sandi was already on her nerves and her insensitivity grated.

"I most certainly care," she said, "if someone I know is that underhanded it leaves me wondering whom I can trust. I've known Conrad for as long as I taught at Fannie Jackson. You would think he would have said something."

Disgusted, Rafiq shook his head. "Unfortunately, he wasn't a true friend. Could he have been the one to call the newspaper? Maybe he sent that tape to Harvey."

Desiree didn't want to believe that a man she'd shared so many confidences with about their respective schools would intentionally want to hurt her.

"Why would Conrad call the paper? I'd already been let go. There was nothing to gain."

"He might still have perceived you as a threat. He wanted to make sure you left Bethesda."

"Puhlease," Sandi piped up. "Why would some candidate for a stupid position be so vindictive? I'm hungry. I'm going to put the pasta up."

She unfolded her long legs and quickly departed.

Desiree wasn't sorry to see her leave. Suddenly the couch shrank in size and a warm, tingly flutter began in the base of her gut and made its way upward, settling in her cheeks. Impossible. She couldn't be attracted to Rafiq.

Desiree had always thought of him as way too uptight and a tad bit stuffy. She'd thought of him as sanctimonious. He reminded her a lot of her father, and she'd suspected he had secrets to hide.

"So what's going on at Fannie Jackson?" she asked, hoping to cover up her reaction. "Any good dirt other than my fall from grace?"

Rafiq chuckled and placed his arm on the back of the couch right behind the nape of her neck. "You're asking the wrong person. I'm not exactly in the loop. I go in, do my job and leave."

"Yes, I noticed. I always thought you were a bit standoffish."

Rafiq's fingers briefly caressed the nape of her neck. "Did you, now?"

She was surprised to discover the spot where he touched her warmed right up. Feeling the need to put distance between them, she stood up abruptly. "Shall we check on Sandi and our dinner?"

She headed off to the kitchen, Rafiq trailing behind her.

After the meal was served and eaten, Sandi, who'd made sure she was practically seated on top of Rafiq, piped up. "Oh, I forgot to mention, you had another call from Tanya."

Desiree exhaled an exasperated sigh. This living arrangement was really beginning to get to her. Sandi had commandeered the answering machine. This wasn't the first time she'd forgotten to give Desiree a message.

"When did she call? And did she say what she wanted?" Her tone came out snippier than she'd intended.

"Yesterday, I think." Sandi didn't sound the least bit contrite.

"You think?"

"Who's Tanya?" Rafiq asked, probably picking up on the tension and hoping to ease it.

"Desiree's sister," Sandi responded, looking up at him adoringly. "Desiree's father's ill. We're guessing that's probably why Tanya's calling."

Rafiq now remained silent, looking from one to the other.

"What was the message?" Desiree asked, guilt at not returning the initial call now consuming her.

"I don't know. She just left her number again and asked that you call her back. I'm thinking maybe you should. She did sound a bit frantic."

Rafiq was still quietly listening, but kept his own counsel.

No point in belaboring the situation. Not with a guest present. "I'll put coffee on," Desiree volunteered, standing. She forced a brightness she did not feel into her voice. "Anyone for dessert? The choices are chocolate cake or flan."

"I'll take coffee, black. Gotta watch my girlish fig-ure," Sandi chimed in, not offering to help.

"Coffee sounds good and chocolate cake sounds like something the doctor ordered. Do you need help?" Rafiq offered, rising to join her.

Desiree saw this as the perfect opportunity to speak to him in private about this mysterious proposition of his. She ignored the pleading look Sandi threw her.

"Yes, sure. You can help with the mugs and plates and we can have our chat in private."

As she moved off toward the kitchen, the phone rang again.

"You can answer or ignore it," Desiree said to the woman she no longer thought of as her friend.

CHAPTER 9

"I can't believe Desiree hasn't returned your call," Ella said grumpily. "I brought that child up better than that. Now she's acting as if she has no family."

"It's been years since we laid eyes on her. We're no longer her family, Ma," Tanya reminded dryly.

"What do you mean we're no longer Desiree's family? We're blood. When it comes down to it that has to count for something."

"Desiree's carved out a life for herself. We aren't a part of that life, Mother," Tanya snapped. "Better get over it."

Ella took a sip of her cooling coffee. It tasted like flavored sugar water. She grimaced and set the cup down on the table in front of her.

Looking around the hospital's cafeteria always made

her slightly depressed. It was where families came to while away time and wait for news that more often than not was bad. She spent a lot of her time here these days getting her fix of caffeine. Today she was taking a much-needed break. Terrence required almost round-the-clock watching. His condition, though stable, was not considered good enough to warrant his release from intensive care.

She'd been told by his doctors that his next stroke, if there was a next one, might be fatal. Ella had been asked to get Terrence's affairs in order and gather their children. She'd gone a step further, just in case. She'd contacted their pastor, a good friend, and asked him to remain close by in case she needed him.

"Maybe I should call Desiree myself," Ella said, making up her mind. "Maybe if she heard my voice she'd be responsive."

"Whatever you think best. Use my cell phone, Mother," Tanya said somewhat impatiently, thrusting a tiny silver device at Ella. "I preprogrammed the number. You just have to hit this one button."

Ella's fingers curled around the phone. She'd never been big on newfangled pieces of equipment, but she felt Desiree needed to know that her father might die. She owed the child that much. Terrence Senior, in lucid moments, had also been asking for his daughter. That was amazing, since he had pretty much written off his youngest once she left home.

"It's going to feel so strange talking to Desiree," Ella said more to herself than to Tanya.

"That's providing she answers," Tanya reminded her sourly. "Don't forget, I already left two messages and she hasn't called back."

"Maybe she didn't get them."

"Hmmph!"

Ella took another sip of the tasteless coffee, braced her shoulders and punched the number.

The phone rang for what seemed an eternity, then was finally picked up.

"Who's calling?" Sandi asked through the crackle of long-distance static. The voice on the other end was female, but Sandi made out the woman was asking for Desiree.

"Desiree, is that you?" the woman repeated.

"No, it's her friend, Sandi."

"Is Desiree home?"

"Who's calling? I can relay a message," Sandi said firmly.

Sandi was able to make out words that sounded like "It's her mother."

Desiree simultaneously whispered behind her, "Who is it?"

After covering the mouthpiece, Sandi held the receiver out. "It's for you. It might be your mother."

Desiree remained frozen in her tracks, as if even the act of reaching for the phone was too much. Sandi had to practically shove it into her hand. Rafiq, who'd followed her out of the kitchen, stood quietly watching.

Desiree sounded as if she might be hyperventilating. She heaved in a series of breaths and slowly brought the receiver to her ear.

"Hello," she said, her voice shaky.

Sandi, noticing her shaking hand, moved away, and gestured for Rafiq to follow her into the kitchen.

When they were seated at the kitchen counter he said, "Desiree seemed very upset. I hope her dad's okay."

"She just needs space. How did you know Terrence Mason was her father?"

Rafiq hiked an eyebrow, but let the question slide.

"Desiree's been estranged from her parents for years."

"Estranged as in they don't talk to each other?"

"You've got that right. It's a very old story."

Rafiq appeared deep in thought. His expression revealed he was clearly puzzled. "Desiree's been going through all these life changes without the support of her family?" The eyebrow rose again.

Sandi bristled. What did he think she was, chopped liver? "She's got me," she said. "I've been here for her. I've always been here for her."

"Yes, but you aren't exactly family," Rafiq pointed out.

"I'm the closest thing to family Desiree has."

He hooked a finger through his coffee cup and carefully took a sip of the brew. "How long have you known each other?"

"Years. An eternity. Desiree and I go a long way back. This isn't the first time we've roomed together."

"How did you meet?" Rafiq asked his light-colored eyes fixed on her. Sandi wondered why the history of their relationship was so important to him. But it was hard to avoid a question that direct.

"We were both in our teens and unemployed. We'd read in some newspaper they were looking for young women with star potential, and we auditioned with hundreds of other hopefuls."

"And did you get hired?"

"Yes. We got to talking and found we had a lot in common. We were both runaways."

"You both ran away from home?"

It sounded as if he might need to digest that one.

"Yes, that's right."

The eyebrow rose again. "You were how old?"

"Seventeen, but we looked older. That worked to our advantage."

"But Desiree seems to have a good head on her shoulders. She's responsible." Rafiq spoke as if to himself.

What did responsibly have to do with anything? Why were they wasting time talking about Desiree anyway? She was here and ready for the plucking and she wasn't used to being ignored. Maybe turning up the heat might not be a bad idea after all. Sandi edged her stool next to Rafiq and placed a hand on his sleeve.

"I've been wanting to ask if you're married. Not that it really matters to me."

"Huh?" Rafiq appeared perplexed at the question. He blinked at her as if she were an alien. "I'm divorced, if that's what you're asking."

"What about a girlfriend? Anyone special?"

"Where is this leading?" he asked uneasily.

The man was dense.

Sandi let her fingers trail the length of his arm. "What I'm asking is, would you be interested in going out with me?"

Rafiq pulled his arm away and tucked his hand in his pants pocket.

No man ever turned Sandi down unless they were gay. Men were usually salivating to go out with her. She was, after all, a celebrity, a woman to be wooed and courted. Most men were proud to have her by their side.

"As a friend? Sure, why not."

"And if I wanted more?"

Sandi wound an arm around Rafiq's neck, pretty much forcing him to look at her. She did not want him to mistake her meaning.

"Shouldn't we have dinner first?" he joked.

But she hadn't meant the question as a joke. She'd straighten him out right away.

"What day did you have in mind?"

"Let me check my calendar and get back to you."

Was he serious or just playing with her? Too late, before Sandi could think of a witty comeback, something to keep things light, Desiree joined them in the kitchen. Her friend looked as if she'd been run over by a Mack truck.

Rafiq hopped off his stool. He was at her side in an instant.

"Sandi, get Desiree some water," he said as if she was a servant girl. He took Desiree's arm and led her to the seat he'd vacated. "Here, you sit."

"I don't need to sit. All right, okay, if you insist."

"What did your mother want?" Sandi asked, annoyed at the interruption and the poor timing. "How is your father?" She put herself on automatic. These were all questions she was supposed to ask.

"Things are touch and go with my father," Desiree answered, sounding weary. "He's had a series of small strokes. The doctor thinks the next one might be fatal."

"Then you should be packing, not talking to us," Rafiq said firmly. "I'll help you book a flight and gladly drive you to the airport if you'd like."

Desiree, still appearing stunned, acknowledged his offer with a nod. "Thanks. It's very nice of you to offer, but I'm not quite sure what I'm doing yet. I'll have to think about it."

"Nothing to think about. You have to go home. What if your father dies? You won't be able to live with yourself."

"You don't understand," she said so softly they both barely heard her.

"Understand nothing. Your father's in the hospital and

your mother clearly needs you," he said, taking over. "Sandi, help Desiree pack."

"I'm not sure I can do this. I'm not sure I'm ready to see my family," she mumbled, but still remained seated.

Desiree seemed to have forgotten the people around her and appeared dazed and confused. Rafiq apparently liked that vulnerable state. He was a caregiver, Sandi decided, a man who came into his own when a woman was needy.

"Okay, let's take a walk and talk about it." Rafiq proposed. "Fresh air might do you good and we can figure out what to do. Sandi, get Desiree her coat."

"Desiree can get her coat herself," she heard herself say.

"Yes, I can," Desiree responded, bolting upright and apparently back to normal. She headed for the closet.

Sandi somehow managed to smile. "I take it I'm not invited on this walk," she said. "I'm busy anyway. I need to return some calls. Make sure Desiree takes her key with her. I'll probably be in bed when you get back."

Quickly, she kissed Rafiq on the cheek and headed off, muttering under her breath.

Outside, the air was brisk and a cool crisp night greeted them. A hint of an orangey moon lighted the shady pathways. They'd been walking for almost ten minutes in silence when Rafiq slowed his steps.

"Let's sit," he said, pointing to the park bench nearest to them. The bench was set back from the road and sheltered by shady oak trees, some of which had begun to bud. He used the palm of his hand to brush off fallen leaves and waited for Desiree to take a seat.

Feeling less dazed, she eased onto the seat and waited for him to join her.

"What is it you wanted to talk to me about?" she asked, coming out of her trance.

"My project." Rafiq began to explain about his book. "I don't seem to be making progress and I'd be willing to pay. Nothing close to what you were making, but it's something. It might pay a utility or buy groceries." He laughed deprecatingly.

"Sounds interesting. You've got my attention."

Rafiq told her more about his book. "You could help organize my notes."

"I would never have guessed you're an author," she said, sounding awed, and looking at him as if he'd climbed a notch in her estimation.

Rafiq chuckled heartily as if enjoying a private joke. "I wouldn't exactly call myself that. It's hardly the great American novel, although at times I've referred to it as such. But it's a promise I made to myself."

"So what else can I do? Organizing notes shouldn't take me long."

"You can help with research." Rafiq then went on to describe several other things he had in mind. Desiree wondered why writing what seemed to her a depressing tale was so important to him. She sensed there was a story behind the story.

"What is it about the bipolar personality that fascinates you?" she asked, giving in to her need to know.

Rafiq's body language told her she was treading on sensitive territory. He took his time answering and seemed to be picking his words.

"I had a bipolar son," he admitted.

"Had? Doesn't sound good."

"It's not good. He died."

She heard the hurt in his voice and her heart broke for him. "I know what it's like to lose a child," she said softly. "Assuming you were married, your wife must have been devastated."

"I was married for sixteen years. And, yes, my wife—ex, that is—was devastated. I don't think she will ever fully recover. Our relationship was in trouble for a long time. It didn't survive John's death."

Desiree ran her fingers down the length of his arm. "Can I ask how your son died?"

The pause that followed was almost painful, and then Rafiq said, "John hanged himself. Liz and I had no idea how much pain he was in up until then. We beat ourselves up for a long time after he passed away. No amount of therapy seemed to help."

"Oh, Rafiq" was the only thing she could find to say.

She reached out to hug him, hoping that gesture might bring him some comfort. She sensed he needed that hug.

The loss of her job was nothing compared with his pain. As hopeless as she felt at times, she'd never considered killing herself—well maybe once, but she'd been young and stupid and the desire soon passed. She was a survivor. Tough.

Rafiq's arms twined around her neck. He seemed to enjoy being held. His head rested on her shoulder and she rocked him in her arms, hoping that her show of comfort might help. One hand idly stroked tight curls back from his forehead.

"How long has it been since your son's death?" she asked, thinking that this was becoming too intimate and maybe it would be good to keep him talking.

"Three years and fifteen days. And there's not a day that goes by that I don't think of John and wonder what was so painful in his life."

"He left no note?"

"None that we could find. We knew he had problems. His behavior was erratic at best. When he was diagnosed with bipolar disorder we sought the advice of some of the best doctors. We even tried experimental drugs. Most stabilized his behavior for a short time."

"You mentioned you didn't handle this alone. You sought help."

When Rafiq raised his head Desiree saw the anguish in his eyes. God, she wished she could take away some of his pain. She'd been there. It had been awful. Her fingers massaged his temples and a sigh wrenched free from deep within his gut.

"God, I've missed a woman's touch," he said quietly.

Desiree never saw the kiss coming. It started out as a tentative brushing of her lips then quickly escalated to a deep, sensual exploration. There was the usual push and pull before their tongues melded and their breathing synchronized. Feelings that Desiree didn't dare explore quickly surfaced. While her brain couldn't assimilate how they'd gotten here, it felt right. Natural.

After another soul-shattering kiss they separated. Rafiq looked as bewildered as she felt. They sat afterward for what seemed an eternity because there was no voice to put to the wonder of it all. Finally Rafiq was the one to break the passion-filled silence. "Who would have thought, Desiree? Who would have thought?"

"Yes, who would have thought?" Desiree repeated, in a dreamy voice that didn't sound like her own.

Rafiq opened his arms and Desiree slid into them. She rested her head on his chest and inhaled the tangy smell of a cologne that smelled familiar.

"Go home and make peace with your family," Rafiq urged her. "Family is important even though they can be a pain at times. When you get back we'll talk more about you working for me. If getting a ticket's a problem, I'll give you my miles."

Though she doubted there would be time to retrieve them, it was sweet of him to offer the frequent flier miles that he'd saved. She had credit cards, some dangerously close to their limits, but she should at least be able to charge a ticket.

Maybe she would go home and make peace.

CHAPTER 10

To hell with turning in for the evening, Sandi decided. Not while she was still wide awake and could make some calls and see who might be interested in asking her out.

Mentally, she ticked off the list of possibilities. It seemed fairly obvious that Rafiq Jones wasn't interested in her, and that was definitely his loss. Even so, she couldn't imagine why he was fascinated with Desiree. She was prettier by far and had the more voluptuous body. Desiree had one of those long, lean bodies that wore clothes well, but she could hardly be described as sexy.

You couldn't account for taste, Sandi supposed. Then again, Rafiq's interest in Desiree might have absolutely nothing to do with an attraction. Rafiq might very well have his own agenda. Maybe he just thought Desiree was useful. In her current state she was vulnerable and he might very well be thinking of pumping her to get the inside scoop on Fannie Jackson. Her knowledge could further his cause and give him an edge.

Who could Sandi call? The number of men she had met since arriving in Bethesda was pitiful. She considered the man she'd met at the airport. He was a definite possibility. He'd made his interest known and might jump at the chance of taking her out. She still had his business card, and the cell number he'd scribbled on the back.

There was also Byron. Calling him might prove interesting. Desiree had made it clear she no longer wanted any part of him and would probably not care. Sandi thought she was somewhat shortsighted. What woman in her right mind would let someone like Byron go? He'd made an attempt at reconciliation and Desiree should have welcomed him back with open arms. He was only human, after all, and he'd made a mistake. Desiree should have gotten over his little indiscretion and moved on.

Both Byron's cell and phone numbers were still written on the memo board in the kitchen. All Sandi needed to do was pick up the phone and dial.

She located the cordless phone, poured a glass of wine and made herself comfortable on the couch before punching in the numbers. The phone rang three times before it was picked up.

"Byron Fisher."

It was after nine in the evening but Byron still sounded

formal, as if he were in the office conducting business. Privately, Sandi thought he and Desiree were very similar; both were uptight and needed to loosen up.

Desiree hadn't always been this way. In her late teens she'd been a wild woman who could party with the best of them. Sandi had been surprised to discover who her parents were and that had only been divulged during a late night talk when much too much wine had been consumed.

Sandi understood perfectly why Desiree had chosen to rebel. Her own parents were also pretty well off and for years she'd had no idea what it was to be black and disadvantaged. What she'd experienced growing up was a father who used his money to control his family, especially her mother. It had always been his way or the highway. And as time went on he'd become increasingly more verbally abusive. She and Desiree were two peas in a pod.

"Fisher," Byron repeated shaking her out of her reverie.

Sandi rallied. "I hope I'm not calling too late."

"Who is this?"

Naturally he wouldn't recognize her voice.

"Sandi Thomas," she said in the voice she'd been told was both sultry and warm.

She could almost hear the wheels turning in Byron's head.

"Desiree's friend," she elaborated.

"The friend who is staying with her?"

"Yes, that's me."

A huge pause followed as he waited for her to go on. Then he asked, "Is Desiree okay? Is there a problem? Why did she ask you to call me?"

He still wasn't getting it.

"Desiree didn't ask me to call. She's out on a date and, since we met briefly, I thought you might be able to give me some advice."

Okay, so Desiree wasn't exactly out on a date, and she'd bent the truth a bit. But the fact that Desiree and Rafiq hadn't asked her to join them had pissed her off.

"Desiree's dating someone?" Byron asked, sounding perplexed. "When did that happen?

Sandi groaned. "You didn't know? She and Rafiq Jones have gotten friendly. They might have bonded while teaching at Fannie Jackson."

"Hmm."

She wasn't sure how to interpret that grunt. Let him think about it a bit.

"That's not why I'm calling," Sandi said quickly, "you're a pretty together guy and Desiree has always spoken rather highly of you. I'm going to be here for a while and I'm hoping you can give me pointers on how to meet professionals in the area." Sandi let out a long, breathy sigh. "Specifically, I'm hoping to meet men, embarrassing as that might sound. Could we meet up for a drink and talk about this?"

Byron, based on his lengthy pause, seemed to be considering it. "Why not?" he finally said. "I can drop by in a few minutes if you would like."

Perfect. She couldn't have asked for anything better.

"I'd love it," she gushed. "And tell you what? I'll have whatever you like to drink waiting."

"Now that sounds tempting. I'll be over in half an hour, and please don't fuss."

After Sandi hung up she glanced at the wall clock, confirming she had time to freshen up. She smiled thinking she'd like to be a fly on the wall if Desiree just happened to return as Byron was arriving. If she walked in with Rafiq after Sandi and Byron were seated on the couch, that would be even better.

Carefully, she went through the closet, choosing a pair of low-rise jeans that did justice to her butt. She pulled on a cropped shirt in cherry-red which revealed a hint of sepia skin where the waistband and top didn't quite meet. Running her fingers through her hair, she gave a quick glance in the mirror. The end results were just as she'd hoped. She did look a bit wicked. Quickly, she applied a bronzer to her face and neck, then added a dash of cherry-red lipstick that made her look hot. Now she was quite ready to take on the world and Byron Fisher.

As she walked back into the kitchen, she noted that Desiree and Rafiq still hadn't returned. Their walk was turning out to be a rather long one. Sandi searched through the cupboards and refrigerator, found crackers and cheese, and set about arranging a tempting platter, adding strawberries for good measure.

Just as she was finishing up, the doorbell rang. She practically flew to answer and pasting an inviting smile on her face, threw open the door.

"Hi, Byron. You got here quickly." Sandi offered her cheek up for his kiss.

Byron surprised her by wrapping his arms around her shoulders and hugging her close.

"I'm glad you called," he said when he released her.

"I'm glad I did, too." Her hand lingered a bit longer than necessary on his arm, stroking the expensive material of his Burberry coat.

So far things were moving along nicely, even better than she'd expected.

Sandi gestured to the couch covered with throw pillows. "Make yourself comfortable, Byron, I'll get us something to drink. How does wine sound?"

"Red would be great if you have it. It's supposed to be good for the heart."

Red? He would have to ask for that. White would have been easier; there was an abundance in the refrigerator. But red, well, hopefully Desiree had some stashed in one of those cupboards.

"What's your second choice?" Sandi countered.

"Absolut and tonic."

That would be another challenge. Who knew if Desiree had high-priced vodka stashed in that liquor cabinet of hers?

After excusing herself, she scurried around looking for red wine and vodka. Red wine was found in a rack, a label she didn't recognize, but it would have to do.

She poured the wine into two glasses and returned to the living room to find Byron seated on the couch. He'd used the time to find a CD and pop it into the stereo. Now the sultry tunes of the latest Anita Baker release wafted its way over. Byron rose and relieved her of one of the glasses. He took her hand and guided her back toward the couch.

"I just love Anita Baker," he said. "I'm thrilled she's making a comeback."

Sandi nodded, hoping her ignorance didn't show. She'd listened to Anita almost a decade ago. The singer's voice was unforgettable. She wasn't much into nostalgia and was more inclined to listen to talent like Alicia Keyes and Usher.

"You and I have a lot in common," Byron said, draping an arm around the back of the couch, his fingers making light circles on her nape. Yup, the boy was a player all right, he had the moves down pat. "Desiree has mentioned you before. You were the friend who moved to Europe and made a name for herself there."

"I suppose you could say that."

Byron squeezed her shoulder. "Don't be so modest. You're a big movie star in Europe."

He should only know that she'd been fired from her last movie. Supposedly, she'd been too demanding. The only way she had a prayer at collecting what they owed her was to take the producer, Milo Valencia, to court.

Byron had at least been gracious enough not to mention that her claim to fame was soft porn. Or maybe it wasn't graciousness; maybe he really didn't know that's how she made her living.

Sandi looked at the time flashing from the CD console. It was way after ten and still no sign of Rafiq and Desiree. As unlikely as it might seem, things had probably heated up between the two, maybe they were planning on spending the night together.

"Sandi," Byron said, "you're a million miles away."

"Sorry. Just thinking."

"Thinking of meeting professional men in the area?" He joked. "Why look any further? You've met me."

Sandi sighed deeply. "Professional doesn't necessarily mean single. To tell you the truth I'm a little uncomfortable, since you and Desiree share a past."

Byron's fingers kneaded the flesh at the back of her neck. "And that's all in the past. Since I'm not promised to anyone I am free to consider a future. Desiree was given every chance possible to patch up our little disagreement. She didn't want to. She didn't want me."

"Even if that's the case, how would it look if her new roomie became involved with her old man?"

"I don't care how it looks, do you?"

Before she could answer, Byron bent over and kissed her.

The intensity of his kiss took Sandi by surprise. She responded like a woman thirsty for water, drinking him in. And after they separated, she felt unfulfilled. For far too long she'd denied herself human touch. In Europe, not a day went by that she wasn't making love and not necessarily with the same partner. Europeans knew how to live and had their priorities in order. Americans, in comparison, were uptight and almost puritanical.

"That was nice," Byron whispered, his voice husky with desire, his breathing uneven. "I say we change locations and go to my place."

Why not? If she went home with Byron she wouldn't have to deal with Desiree and Rafiq's return, and the astonished looks on their faces. She wouldn't have to feel chastised or like some kind of a pariah.

As if to persuade her, Byron kissed her again. This time he pressed his body against the length of hers and she could feel his desire take a tangible form. While he might come off as straightlaced, he seemed to know his way around the female anatomy rather comfortably.

"Let's go," he repeated.

"Just let me grab a few things and we'll be on our way."

Sandi left him for the bedroom, where she shoved some cosmetics in a bag and hurriedly grabbed a change of underwear. When she was almost through she heard the sound of voices coming from outside. Desiree and Rafiq had returned. Their timing couldn't be better.

Her sole priority now was to get Byron out of that house as quickly as humanly possible. She breezed in to the living room preparing to do just that.

"Hey, guys," she said. "I was just about to send a search party out for you. You've been gone quite a while. Byron stopped by in your absence and we got to chatting...."

"Yes, I noticed," Desiree said, her voice even, and her expression not revealing a thing.

"Well, we didn't want to leave until you got back. Now that you're here, we're on our way. Coming, Byron?"

Byron was already standing with his Burberry coat on. He nodded in Desiree and Rafiq's direction.

"Nice seeing you both. Don't wait up for Sandi."

With that, he whisked her out the front door.

CHAPTER 11

"Is that woman really a friend?" Rafiq asked the moment the door shut behind Sandi and Byron. "Heaven help you if she is." He rolled his eyes as if to emphasize his point.

Desiree shrugged, though inwardly she was seething. She and Byron were over, but she still couldn't believe he'd had the audacity to stop by and make himself comfortable when she was out. Even more upsetting was Sandi's obvious disrespect for her.

"I've known Sandi a long time," Desiree answered, keeping her voice neutral. "Nothing she does surprises me anymore."

"How come you're allowing her to stay with you, then?"

"She asked. I couldn't turn her down," Desiree explained.

That should be good enough for now. It was all he needed to know. She refused to admit that it still hurt to see Byron. Desiree did feel betrayed but it was useless moaning about loyalty and feelings of obligation.

"It's none of my business," Rafiq said, as if sensing her inward struggle. "With friends like her, you'd be better off keeping your enemies close to your bosom."

Desiree tried to make light of it. She even managed a chuckle. It came out sounding more like a sob. "I take it you don't like her?"

"I don't dislike her," Rafiq said, still standing. "I'm just not sure I trust her. Listen, I'm going to take off and leave you to pack. You'll be leaving for Atlanta tomorrow and you need a good night's sleep."

Desiree groaned. "Yes, I suppose, though I am dreading going."

"You'll feel much better if you get it over with."

She nodded, though she doubted going to Atlanta would make her feel better. Seeing her family was bound to be tough. Too many memories would be dredged up, few of them pleasant. And the trip would cost her plenty, cutting into her already dwindling funds. Buying a plane ticket at the last minute would be exorbitant.

Desiree said goodbye to Rafiq at the door. He held her close to him for a moment and whispered in her ear, "Hurry back so that we can get started on that project we discussed."

Despite the niggling worry that Rafiq might have his own agenda, it still felt good to be needed. It felt even better knowing he'd offered her a job.

"What a fabulous place you have," Sandi commented, trailing a manicured hand across Byron's butter-soft leather couch. Her gaze did not miss the burgundy velvet throw draped over the back of it. It smacked of a woman's touch. Desiree's, maybe.

The inside of Byron's home was truly magnificent. She took in the vaulted ceilings and the unlit stone fireplace with the assortment of candles arranged on the mantel.

"Thanks," Byron said. "I did have help decorating. You like it?"

Sandi's eyes narrowed. "You hired a professional to do all of this? It must have cost you a bundle."

Byron shook his head. "No, Desiree had…I mean has excellent taste. I let her do whatever she wanted."

Sandi felt herself go still inside. She hadn't known Desiree and Byron had been that serious. She wondered if Byron was still hung up on Desiree. He had tried to get her back. Most men would have already found a replacement.

"Show me the rest of the place," Sandi said boldly. "I'd especially like to see where you sleep."

For a brief moment Byron's jaw muscle twitched; the only visible sign of any emotion. Sandi wasn't sure how to interpret that. *It is what it is,* she thought when he took her by the hand and said, "Eating and dining over here." He pointed out a well-appointed galley kitchen off to the side.

The cherrywood cabinets were an artisan's work and the charming dining nook with seating for four, off to the right, looked comfortable.

Still holding her by the hand, Byron led her up a long hallway. He stopped briefly to flip on a light and she followed him into a medium-sized bathroom. The walls were painted coffee and cream, and chocolate-brown towels with gold logos declared it a masculine haven.

"Nice," Sandi said, even though her throat felt as if she'd swallowed grit. "Did Desiree decorate this, too?"

One of Byron's eyebrows hiked. "She did, as a matter of fact, and with very little direction from me. Desiree knew exactly what I liked."

She bet. Sandi was still trying to assess how deep Byron's feelings ran for her roommate. Not that it much mattered now. By the time she was done with him, she would be the only female that he'd be able to think about.

Byron continued on, the heels of his polished Cole Haans thudding against the wooden floor. After climbing three little steps, they entered a spacious room that held a king-size bed with a hand carved headboard and footboard. Louvered shutters painted an attractive sand and green took the place of curtains at the windows. The plank floors held beige and burgundy rugs arranged in no particular fashion.

An especially plush rug lay before the copper fireplace

and, in one far corner, a computer table with a comfortable swivel chair faced outward to look onto what must be a patio.

Outside, the soft sounds of rain pattered against the windowpanes.

"I love your home," Sandi said, deliberately gushing as she released Byron's hand to rush toward the fireplace. "Can you start a fire? It's been ages since I sat before a real fireplace."

"Certainly, if that's what you'd like."

As Byron bent over to gather a starter log and ignite it with matches, Sandi admired his athletic body. There wasn't a bulge of fat on him; it was clear he worked out. A wide smile surfaced as she visualized the sinewy muscle that lay under his conservative chinos and Brooks Brothers shirt. She was determined that, before the evening ended, she would unravel all his mysteries.

Soon the room was filled with a golden glow and the smell of hickory tickled her nostrils. Sandi removed the embroidered shawl she'd draped over one shoulder. She dangled it off the tip of one finger and with her free hand stroked the column of her neck.

"Wheeew! It's gotten quite warm all of a sudden."

"Is that a hint that you've had enough of the fire?" Byron asked.

"No, it's a hint I'd like something cool to drink."

"Ah, where are my manners?"

Byron offered up a rare smile. When he left her, Sandi

lowered herself onto one of the rugs. She made sure her hair fanned out behind her as she stared into what was quickly becoming a roaring fire. How to play this? Byron wasn't big on aggressive females, she sensed. He would want to do things on his terms. His way.

Sandi kicked off the stiletto heels that were her signature. She wiggled her toes confined in expensive hose then lay back to enjoy the woodsy scent of the fire. When she heard Byron approach behind her, she pretended she was unaware of his presence.

He cleared his throat before sliding down to join her, his long legs splayed out before him and he handed her one of the two brandy snifters he held. So much for cool drinks. Things were quickly warming up.

"What is this?" Sandi asked inhaling the pungent scent of a liqueur that was familiar yet foreign.

"Courvoisier."

Byron made it sound as if it was no big deal, something the average Joe kept in his liquor cabinet.

"Smells wicked and exotic," Sandi said, her fingers curling around the glass.

Now they sat staring at the crackling fire, each lost in their own thoughts, Sandi's leg occasionally brushing against Byron's. After about five minutes of uninterrupted silence Byron rose to put a disk in the CD.

It was music designed to soothe the soul.

"Beyoncé!" Sandi exclaimed, pleasantly surprised at Byron's taste in music. "Excellent choice."

Her enthusiasm seemed to break the ice and Byron returned to wrap a sinewy arm around her shoulders. "Glad I'm able to please."

She lay her head on his broad shoulders and closed her eyes, inhaling the very masculine smell of him. While she hummed along to the music, the back of Byron's hand grazed her cheek. Needing no further encouragement she cuddled up against him.

"I'm so comfortable with you," Sandi purred.

"And I with you. You're beautiful. No, stunning, and you put people at ease."

"Thank you. If I had put my wishes on paper and sent it out to the universe you would be it."

"I'm flattered," Byron said, flashing her another smile. "Maybe we should get more comfortable?"

He'd given her the perfect opening. Things were moving along nicely.

"I thought you would never ask."

Byron was already whipping off his shoes and unbuttoning his shirt. In seconds he'd stripped down to his undershirt, though it still remained tucked in his slacks. Sandi got a glimpse of a body that appeared flawless and signified that the gym might be his second home. Her eyes were drawn like magnets to his biceps, which looked as if they were hewn out of marble. What would it feel like to have those powerful arms around her and be locked against those hips?

If she had anything to do with it, she would know soon.

When Byron kissed her, Sandi took the lead and deepened the kiss. She wound her arms around his neck and planted her breasts firmly against his chest. How much clearer could she make it that she was totally into him? He might choose to ignore the signals, but if that were the case, it would be better to know what she was up against now.

Byron's hands kneaded her back muscles. His tongue circled her mouth, exploring. Sandi's breath hitched when he straddled her and successfully pinned her body to the floor. In a few short seconds things had gotten even hotter.

From a distance, Sandi heard firewood crackle and logs on the verge of falling apart hiss and snap. The scent of burning wood now warred with the heat of a man on fire. When Byron's hands slid under Sandi's shirt and his fingers made circles against her skin, she groaned. She wished he would touch her all over.

"Maybe we should take this to the bed?" Byron said.

"Maybe we should," Sandi responded, boldly running her palm over what had now become an obvious bulge in his pants.

With some reluctance, Byron moved off of her, allowing her to rise.

He quickly began shedding his clothing and Sandi followed suit. By the time they climbed into bed they were both naked as the day they were born.

Byron lay on his back and gestured for Sandi to sit on top of him. She did so, leaning in slightly so that he had full access to her breasts. She wove her fingers through his chest hairs as he circled her nipple with one hand then took that same nipple into his mouth.

Byron's free hand cupped her buttocks, positioning her against his shaft. As the friction built, Sandi felt heat suffuse her face and electric jolts ricochet through her body, making her toes curl. She wanted him inside of her, wanted to feel every inch of him. Byron, sensing her need, shifted and made himself more accessible.

"Hop on, baby," he said.

And Sandi did, throwing her head back and lowering herself onto him until she was totally impaled.

Byron began rhythmic pumping that made Sandi gasp. She was bouncing up and down, Byron orchestrating every move with a light touch of his hand on her waist.

When his breathing turned into pants and the intensity of the rhythm picked up, blood roared in Sandi's ears and the pulsing at her core took over. The only rational thought now was to seek relief at any cost.

As Byron pumped away, Sandi pressed into him. She brought his hands to her breasts and made him squeeze her nipples. Eventually she began spiraling out of control as pleasurable sensations took over. She rode the wave, trying her best to wait for a signal from Byron he was ready.

That signal came faster than she expected when with a muffled sound he exploded inside her. Now there was no longer a reason for her to hold back.

Sandi let go, allowing herself to soar. She was conscious of their juices mingling, of tangled limbs and erratic breathing. She was acutely aware that, given they were almost virtual strangers, they'd been good together. No, better than good. They'd been pretty damn wonderful.

CHAPTER 12

Desiree exited the Jetway clutching the one piece of luggage she'd bothered to pack. She had no intention of spending more time than it took to make sure her father's condition was stable. She scanned the area to see if her brother had made it through security. Convinced he had not, she continued on her way.

After an earlier and rather stilted conversation with Tanya that morning, Desiree informed her she would be flying in to Hartsfield-Jackson International Airport. Tanya had then called back to say Terrence would pick her up.

It was not what Desiree wanted, but to decline would be rude. She'd rather take a cab than make small talk with a man who was a virtual stranger. Not that Desiree had anything against Terrence Junior. The age difference between them being what it was, she'd never really gotten to know him. Her only memories were of a withdrawn teenager who'd left for college and never come home.

Although she had no luggage to claim, Desiree headed for the baggage carousel. It made sense that Terrence would be waiting for her there. For a brief moment, her mind ran to Sandi and the closed bedroom door she hadn't bothered to open. Who knew if the woman had even come home?

Desiree approached the baggage area, skirting groups of hovering people. Some looked anxiously up at the digital board waiting for their flight number to flash. She spotted hers and made a beeline for the area.

A scan of the gathering crowd did not yield the tall, bespectacled, self-conscious boy she remembered. There was one man standing off to the side dressed casually in jeans and a windbreaker who might be Terrence. Desiree made her way toward him.

"Terrence?" she called, looking at him uncertainly.

"I'm not Terrence but I'd damn sure like to be."

Desiree managed a rueful smile. The stranger's blatant admiration was salve to her battered ego. After apologizing profusely, she moved on. No one seemed a good fit for the man she remembered.

Then she spotted a forty-something-year-old male hovering behind a potted plant. Could that rather trendy dresser be Terrence? That would be a drastic change. The size of the links of gold the chain around the man's neck must have set him back a couple of paychecks.

Desiree considered approaching him. A young woman in a flashy pair of red patent leather boots and a miniskirt that hugged her butt beat her to it. She embraced him enthusiastically, seeming to forget about the little girl who was holding onto her hand.

A passionate kiss followed. Given the intensity, it should have been saved for a more private moment. But in some ways Desiree envied the couple. How glorious to be in love and oblivious to the world.

"Desiree?"

A deep voice came from behind her. Desiree turned to see a man in an expensive double-breasted suit and bow tie bearing down on her. Who in the world wore bow ties these days, except to black-tie affairs? Then she remembered how stuffy Terrence had always been.

"Terry?" she inquired, smothering the smile that his absurd outfit had produced.

"Terrence." He offered up his cheek for her kiss.

He seemed uptight and awkward, but Desiree dutifully pecked his cheek and clasped him in an embrace that she could tell was unwelcome.

"Is that all your luggage?" Terrence asked, appearing uncomfortable by even that small show of affection.

"It is."

"Can't say I blame you for not planning on staying long."

Desiree changed the subject and asked what was expected of her. "How's Dad?"

Her brother seemed to chew on the question for a while. Taking long strides he headed outside and toward the parking lot. Desiree's legs weren't exactly short but she was having a difficult time catching up.

"I guess he's holding his own," Terrence said after a while.

"You haven't seen him?"

"Why should I? I can't stand the old bastard."

So she wasn't alone in her sentiments, though she'd never had the courage to put it quite like that.

Once seated in Terrence's BMW, she asked, "What about Mom? How is she holding up?"

"As best as can be expected. She practically lives at the hospital and so does Tanya."

As Terrence navigated his way out of the parking lot, Desiree steeled herself for the reunion to come. Seeing Terrence so far hadn't been bad, it was like being seated next to a stranger to whom you were obligated to make small talk.

"I'm surprised Tanya is able to leave her family for such long periods of time," Desiree said.

"I'm sure she has a vested interest."

Desiree eyed her brother warily. "What's that supposed to mean?"

"If the old bastard dies, she'll inherit a bundle."

Desiree tossed Terrence a puzzled look. "Besides the house, and a few dollars in the bank, what do they really have?"

Terrence took his eyes off the road briefly. "Trust me, they're loaded. A lot of it is liquid, too. Since you and I are persona non grata, it's doubtful we'll see a dime."

"*I'm* persona non grata," Desiree corrected. "You, at least, have maintained some type of relationship with them."

"I'd hardly call it that," Terrence said out of the corner of his mouth. "I can't stand the sight of the old buzzard and I've lost all respect for our mother. Beats me why she would put up with his behavior all these years. She'd be better off if he were dead."

Desiree couldn't bring herself to wish anyone dead, though admittedly she'd wished it on Byron, briefly. But curiosity got the better of her.

"Why do you hate our dad so much?"

Terrence responded by stomping on the accelerator. The speedometer climbed to seventy.

"Probably for the exact same reason you do, though you're not voicing it. Isn't that why you left home? Our dad beat the crap out of our mother, and he passes himself off as a God-fearing man."

So Terrence knew what had actually been going on. He'd probably heard the screams at night and noticed the attire chosen to hide the bruises. Seeing her mother again would be reliving the nightmare. Seeing her father would be even worse. She was an adult. She could get through this.

"So how's the lawyering?" Desiree asked Terrence,

who was now hiding his stuffy good looks behind expensive sunglasses.

"Helps put food on the table."

"And you've never married?" she asked, guessing that such a thing might not rank high on Terrence's agenda.

"No."

"Why not?"

With that, Terrence made a quick right and exited off the highway. This time he kept his gaze straight ahead on the road.

"What I've witnessed of that institution leaves a lot to be desired," he mumbled.

"But there are happy couples. There must be," Desiree insisted. She had to believe that; deep down somewhere in her gut she still believed in love.

"Name them," Terrence snapped. "People marry because they want children. I, on the other hand, have no desire to add to an overpopulated world."

Desiree decided it might be wiser to keep her lips buttoned. She was dealing with one angry man. She stared out the window watching the scenery whiz by. Last night seemed a long time ago. She'd made out with a man she hardly knew, a man who'd awakened in her a passion Byron never could. No, she would not think about Rafiq. She needed to prepare herself for what lay ahead.

Despite her resolve, a smile curved her lips. She could picture his face clearly: the deep bronze of his skin, the whiskey-colored eyes that sparkled and the slightly flared nose. The memories of being in Rafiq's arms and of his unexpected kisses warmed her. Her life had certainly taken a turn for the worse, yet she'd felt a spark ignite with a man she still wasn't sure she could trust. She'd have to examine that later.

"We're here," Terrence announced, and none too soon, swinging the car into a circular driveway. He maneuvered around several hospital vehicles that were double-parked.

Had Desiree been paying attention, she would have realized they were heading directly for the hospital. What would be worse, going to the family home with all its painful memories, or facing the family she'd given up, including the father she despised?

There was a war dance going on in her chest, one she was determined to sit out. She would get through this ordeal somehow.

"Aren't you coming in?" she asked Terrence when he showed no signs of getting out of the car.

He glanced at her, his eyes hidden behind the expensive dark glasses. "Don't have time. I have to get back to work. I'm going to court tomorrow and I need to prepare."

Terrence obviously wanted nothing to do with the reunion. He was grateful to have an excuse to hurry off. He was clearly over the family. Still, it would have helped to have him with her.

"But I don't even know which floor Dad's on," Desiree pleaded. She placed one hand on the door handle. "Will I see you later?"

"Sure. Maybe we can have dinner together." His tone was somewhat gentler when he added, "Dad's on the eighth floor. The moment you get off, you'll see the nurses' station. One of them will show you to his room."

Nodding, she stepped out onto the pavement. "You'll need to open the trunk so I can get my bag."

"I'll drop your bag off at the house. Tanya will take you home. Here's my card," he said, flipping the crisp white card at her. "It's got my cell number." With that, Terrence zoomed off.

Desiree was left with little choice but to enter the building. Her stomach threatened to revolt as she swung through the double doors. Hospitals dredged up awful memories of another time and place when a down-and-out teenager was forced to give up a baby. Hospitals she could live without. She'd come to associate them with separation.

The receptionist sitting at a circular desk didn't pay her any mind. Desiree followed the stream of people to the elevator. Closing her eyes briefly, she prepared for the meeting ahead. What did she say to a family she hadn't seen in a lifetime? How could she turn the clock back on twenty-something years?

When she stepped off the elevator, she spotted the nurses' station just as Terrence had said.

"May I help you?" A heavyset African-American nurse

asked, looking up from the chart she was scrutinizing. Her shrewd mud-brown eyes dissected Desiree.

"I'm here to see my…uh Terrence Mason," Desiree answered, flashbacks of another time making the bile rise in her throat.

"Are you family?" The nurse's penciled-in eyebrows hiked.

"Uh, yes. I'm Dr. Mason's daughter."

The woman cocked her head to the side and pursed her lips. "Hmm, I thought he had only one daughter, the one who's here constantly."

What was that supposed to mean? Desiree waited for her to go on.

"He's three doors down, and to the left," the nurse said at last. "Your mother, at least I think she's your mother, is in with him."

"And my sister?"

Desiree needed to know if Tanya was there, too. She needed to prepare herself to face her family: the mother who never quite understood her, and the sister who once encouraged her to be herself but who turned her back on her as the years went by. Recriminations, oh yes, there would be a few.

As she headed down the corridor, Desiree felt determined to make this initial encounter a pleasant one. This was a hospital, after all, and conversations filled with dissension needed to take place at the family home.

She was so deep in thought she didn't notice the older

woman standing in the doorway of a room. Thinking she'd missed her father's room, Desiree came to an abrupt halt and spun around. An immaculately dressed older woman had followed her and stared at her as if she were a ghost.

Tears sparkled in the woman's dark brown eyes then trickled in rivulets down her cheeks. Her eyes remained on Desiree as if unable to believe that she was seeing her in the flesh. Ella's mouth moved but no sound came out. Her mother was heavier than she remembered but, as always, perfectly groomed. Desiree forced herself to cover the distance separating them.

"Hello, Mother."

Ella's face creased into a wider smile. She opened her arms, clearly expecting Desiree to step in.

"Just 'hello, Mother'? Come here, darling, and give me a kiss. It's been a long time. I was worried you wouldn't come. I missed you."

Darling? As the youngest, she had always been her mother's darling. No, no, she couldn't permit the memories to take over. Memories of sitting in her mother's ample lap while they comforted each other, scents of soap and an expensive perfume mingling with the warmth of Ella's flesh.

Desiree allowed herself to be folded into the warm embrace. Ella smelled just as she remembered, a combination of Ivory soap and Chanel. After what Desiree considered to be sufficient time, she gracefully disentangled herself.

"Well, Tanya said you wanted to see me, so here I am," she managed breezily around the lump in her chest.

"Honey, I've dreamed about this for years. Wished it." Ella took a step back, staring into Desiree's face. "You look lovelier than I ever imagined. You are your father's child. You've got that eternally youthful glow. Wait until he sees you, baby. He's been asking for you in his lucid moments."

It was hard to imagine Terrence Senior asking for her after all these years. At times, she'd thought he hated her. Even when she was a child, they'd hardly ever spoken. Her very appearance seemed to set him off.

"How is he?" Desiree forced herself to ask, not able to wrap her tongue around the word *father*.

"Come see for yourself. He needs to see what a beautiful woman you've become. He will be so proud. You can fill us in on the years we've missed." Ella wiped a tear and sniffled.

Searching through her purse, Desiree found a tissue and handed it over. "Where is Tanya?" she asked, not quite ready to come face-to-face with her father.

"She had to go home. She has a husband to feed and two kids who need her. For the last couple of weeks she's spent almost every waking moment here."

Was her mother deliberately trying to make her feel guilty? Too late—she'd given up guilt. She'd paid her dues and would no longer lug that burden around.

"Who did Tanya marry?" Desiree asked, hoping to delay the inevitable.

"Ron Smith. Remember him? He used to follow her around like a puppy dog though she paid him no mind. He's done well for himself. He makes a comfortable living. She doesn't have to work."

"And what does he do?"

"He's a CPA. We can catch up on the family news later. Come see your father. He's been waiting."

Oh, God! She'd come this far. She could do it. This is where her old acting skills would help her.

Ella took her by the hand, practically pulling her into a room that smelled of antiseptic. It was eerily quiet except for the drone of machines that Desiree presumed now kept her father alive.

The figure in bed with his eyes closed did not look like the big strapping man she remembered. A silver-capped head peeked out from under the covers and a gaunt face, the skin stretched tightly across prominent bones, looked skeletal. Terrence Mason's eyes were closed and, except for his shallow breathing, you would not think he was alive.

"Look who's here," her mother said cheerily.

Was that a soft snore, then movement?

"Desiree came to see you," Ella repeated in the same cheery tone. "Our daughter is here."

This time a wheeze came from the bed. Desiree's eyes remained riveted on the frail body covered by ivory linens. Her father's two emaciated arms, a peculiar shade of ageing mahogany, contrasted sharply against the whiteness of the sheets. Her limbs would not cooperate. She was incapable of putting one foot in front of the other.

Ella nudged her. "Come closer so that he can see you. He doesn't have his contacts in."

Taking her hand again, Ella dragged her toward her father's bed.

Desiree steeled herself to look on the man she had both hated and feared. The wasted body, the shell that seemed barely alive, was clearly not the intimidating man she remembered. One side of Terrence Senior's face was grossly distorted, yet he managed to squint open an eye.

"Hello, Father," Desiree said, her voice coming out reed thin. "How are you feeling?"

The one eye he had focused on her didn't even blink. A choking sound came from the distorted mouth, words she couldn't make out.

Ella clapped her hands. "He's responding. He recognizes you. Thank you, Jesus. He hasn't been this alert in days."

Alert isn't what Desiree would have called him. She felt the tears on her lashes and focused her attention on a chest of drawers against the far wall that held vases of flowers. She hadn't expected this, not the wasted body, not a man clearly waiting to die. Seeing him like this made the anger built up over the years dissipate. To think she'd expended her energy hating a weakening old man.

It was time to let bygones be bygones and bury her hatred of a man who was no longer capable of harming her. Desiree covered her father's bony fingers with hers as if by dong so she could inject her energy into him. She swore she felt movement, but wasn't sure. Despite her resolve not to get caught up in emotions, a sob flew from her throat.

"Look, Desiree," Ella said. "Your dad's happy to see you. He's smiling."

It was wishful thinking on her mother's part. Desiree averted her eyes from the grossly distorted mouth. Her father was clearly gasping for air. She doubted he knew who she was and even where he was.

"Shall we let him rest?" Desiree asked, attempting to slide her hand out from under his.

With amazing strength her hand was clutched in a viselike grip. Another gargled sound followed. The one eye Terrence Senior had opened stared directly at her. In her father's own fashion he was attempting to speak.

"He's lucid," Ella said excitedly. "I told you he was happy to see you. You've always been his favorite."

Desiree doubted that was true. She remembered the arguments her failure to conform had produced. Her dad had wanted his children to be perfect. And she'd been far from perfect. She was the underachiever daughter, the embarrassment. Terrence Senior had expected his offspring to toe the line. They had a position in the community to maintain and he'd had Desiree's life mapped out for her. She was to go off to college and major in education or nursing, professions which at that time held little appeal for her. She'd wanted to be an actress, a career her father had frowned on, considering it beneath her. Ironic that after all that fighting she'd ended up getting her act together and establishing herself in a profession he'd approve of.

A petite nurse came breezing in. She carried a tray in her hand.

"Time for Dr. Mason's medicine," she said cheerily. "I'm also going to clean him up a bit."

A rustling noise came from under the covers, followed by another strangled sound. Terrence Senior's grip on Desiree's hand loosened and she was able to slide her fingers out from under his.

The nurse clearly wanted them out so that she could do her thing.

"Maybe we should leave, Mom," Desiree suggested. "Call Tanya and I'll take you both to lunch."

"I shouldn't leave. I mean, I've never left in the middle of the day. What if Terrence should need something?"

"If he does, Mrs. Mason," the nurse piped up, "I can take care of it. Leave your cell phone number so we can reach you."

Reluctantly Ella put on her sweater and gathered her purse. "Tanya should be here any minute," she said. "So there'll be no reason to call."

Again, Desiree regretted not renting a car. It would have allowed her a certain amount of freedom.

"Let's wait for Tanya out front, Mother," Desiree suggested, needing a breath of fresh air.

She took her mother's hand and led her to the elevator.

CHAPTER 13

"Desiree, are you home?" Sandi called, not really expecting an answer. She couldn't blame Desiree for being pissed off at her, but her friend would eventually get over it. In the past she always had.

Sandi had planned to creep back into the condo before sunrise. But somehow she'd managed to oversleep. By the time she'd made love to Byron again and crawled out of bed, it was time for him to go to work.

As she tiptoed toward her bedroom she was conscious of the eerie quietness. That meant Desiree was well on her way to Atlanta and the confrontation could be delayed.

"Desiree!" Sandi called again, just to be sure. "Are you in? Are you sleeping?"

Getting no answer, she felt more confident. No point in tiptoeing around now, not when she had the condominium to herself. She hadn't done anything wrong moving in on Byron. Desiree had made it clear she didn't want the man.

A smart woman did not turn her back on opportunity. With no immediate prospects in sight, Sandi knew her funds were dwindling fast. She'd never been one to save and, with no immediate film prospects lined up, things were looking pretty bad. Thirty-seven was old to be doing these types of films. Today, younger, more brazen women were coming onto that scene. They were willing to work cheaper and do the most outrageous things to make names for themselves.

Sandi, a diva in her own right, had come to expect the perks that went along with star billing. She would not settle for anything less. On the last set, she'd thrown a temper tantrum and doused the starlet with coffee when she'd found out the woman was sleeping with the producer, Milo Valencia. Sandi and Milo Valencia had had an agreement. She took care of his physical needs and he took care of her.

This time, Sandi's impulsive act had gotten her fired. As word traveled fast through the adult entertainment community, she was soon ostracized. She was blackballed and labeled a troublemaker. Now her only hope was to land something in the States.

Hooking up with Byron Fisher could be the answer to a prayer. But she'd make damn sure that he didn't find out how she made a living. Desiree wasn't in a position to rat her out. She had too much to lose.

Sandi had already figured out Byron lived by a double standard. He might enjoy being freaky, but he'd never consider an adult entertainer marriage material, and forget about taking her out in public. Byron was all about making a good impression with his friends. But Sandi planned on hanging on to him. He could very well be her ticket to a different life.

She paused in front of Desiree's closed bedroom door. Sticking her head inside couldn't hurt. When her tentative rap on the door yielded no answer, Sandi's hand fastened around the knob. She stuck her head in and spotted Desiree's made bed. She grimaced. The only indications of a hasty departure were the shoes Desiree had left out.

It still amazed her that anyone could be this anal. Sandi's own room looked like a cyclone had blown through it. Clothes were tossed on every available surface. She even pushed aside piles to climb into bed.

Fatigue was beginning to take its toll as she retraced her steps to the kitchen. She'd get a quick something to eat before she hit the sack. Sandi opened the refrigerator, found a juice carton and took a quick swig. She removed a plate of covered leftovers and noticed for the first time the note on the counter with her name written on it.

Picking it up, she quickly scanned it then read it out loud.

Sandi
I've decided to go to Atlanta. I'll be back as soon as

I can. Take good care of my home and call me if there's a problem. You've got my cell number.

It had finally been confirmed. Desiree was gone, at least temporarily. How ironic that a woman who'd been hell-bent on putting distance between herself and family had caved under pressure!

Sandi's own parents had died a while back. She and her family had never had much of a relationship, but she so needed their approval that she'd sent money and photos back to them anyway. She'd wanted to rub their noses in it, to show them that, despite their lack of support, she'd made it.

Bed was definitely calling now. After she awoke she'd phone Glenn Browne, the man she'd met at the airport. If things didn't work out with Byron, he'd be her ace in the hole. At the very least, he could serve as an entertaining diversion.

"Harvey would like to see you in his office," Ida announced, her booming voice carrying across the teachers' lounge.

Rafiq set down his coffee mug and gave her his full attention. He'd been using the time between classes to outline a particularly difficult chapter of his book.

"Harvey wants to see me now?" Rafiq asked, his own voice modulated. He hoped Ida would get the message and lower her voice as well.

"Yes, right now. He's scheduled pretty tightly today."
Having issued the command, she waited.

The few teachers in the lounge pretended to be busy but Rafiq knew they were all ears. They were all dying to find out who would be Harvey's successor.

"I have class in fifteen minutes," he answered Ida. "There isn't a substitute around."

"I'm sure Harvey knows that," Ida said patiently. "It won't take fifteen minutes, if that."

Resigned to having to meet with Harvey, Rafiq packed up his papers and stood. He followed Ida's mincing steps down the hallway, preparing himself for the worst. There would be few options left if he didn't get this job. He would have to consider moving, something he was not looking forward to. Returning to New Jersey didn't seem feasible. He'd left that life behind.

Phyllis Wright, the Caucasian math teacher brushed by him as he neared Harvey's office. Her face was crimson and she looked visibly distraught.

"Hi, Phyllis. Everything okay?"

She ignored his greeting and continued on her way. Was this a sign of things to come? Had Harvey made a decision at last?

Ida, who'd probably seen everything in her stint as Harvey's assistant, shook her head and led the way. Rafiq followed her into an outer office, noting that Harvey's office door was closed.

"It looks like he's running behind," Ida said. "Have a

seat and I'll try reaching him on the intercom to let him know you are here."

Left with little choice, Rafiq eased himself onto one of the uncomfortable chairs that flanked Harvey's door. His thoughts turned to Desiree. He wondered how she was faring. Going home had to be hard. He remembered their passionate kisses and hoped he hadn't scared her.

She'd responded like a woman interested and he'd dared to hope. But his pursuit of her would have to be handled carefully. He didn't want her thinking that his offer of a job came with strings attached. Attraction aside, Desiree was the perfect person to help with his book. She was organized and efficient and would keep him on track.

Ida now presided behind a desk covered with framed photographs. It was more like a nest. Rafiq had the feeling she didn't have much to do all day beyond fielding calls, typing the occasional letter and keeping her ear to the ground. She must have noticed him staring.

"I can put up coffee if you'd like," Ida offered, though she made no effort to move.

Rafiq tapped the face of his watch. "Thanks, but you don't have time. My class begins in exactly fifteen minutes. Do you think he'll be long?"

At that same moment Harvey's office door opened. Out came a man Rafiq didn't know. He appeared polished and well tailored, clearly comfortable with himself. He nodded in Rafiq's direction and made a beeline for Ida.

"You're to pencil me into Mr. Coleman's first open slot next week."

Ida looked up at him, she didn't seem overly impressed. "It's in accordance with Mr. Coleman's wishes?"

"It is."

"Do as he says, Ida," the dean called, coming out of his office.

Navigating a computer was way beyond Ida's abilities. She flipped open a black appointment book, dug through a drawer and found a pen.

"Name, please."

The man's smile disappeared. "You know it. Conrad Maloney."

"I can't keep track of who comes and goes," Ida said, keeping her eyes trained on the appointment book as she scribbled.

"Rafiq," Harvey boomed, "I'm ready."

Harvey was already walking back the way he had come and clearly expected Rafiq to follow.

Time was ticking away. Rafiq wished he had the luxury of watching the interplay between Conrad and Ida. He would give anything to witness how she handled the outside candidate, the man who was Desiree's friend of convenience, but now he only had ten minutes to have his audience with Harvey. The dean, no doubt, had timed it down to the second.

By the time Rafiq entered The Rack, prepared for Harvey's unique brand of torture, the dean had retreated behind his polished mahogany desk. As was his habit, he steepled his fingers under his chin.

Rafiq patiently waited for him to take the lead. Seconds dragged by before Harvey cleared his throat.

"Let me be perfectly up-front," he said. "I'll be making my decision in a day or two when I get back the results of our background check. There's been a delay "

Rafiq's stomach churned, but he met Harvey's gaze full on. He had to believe that his record was expunged. He'd paid the attorney a goddamn fortune. Hopefully, he'd done his job.

"What happens if Conrad and I both turn out to be squeaky clean?" he asked Harvey.

Harvey unclasped his fingers and turned his palms upward in a helpless gesture. "Then I'll let the board make the final decision."

Easy for Harvey to say. To him it wasn't a big deal. It didn't affect his life one way or the other. But to Rafiq it might mean everything. He'd hoped getting the dean's position would mean stability and some permanence. He'd prayed this would mean the beginning of a new life, a good life.

He needed to let Harvey know that he was serious about this job.

"What can I do to convince you I'm your man?" Rafiq asked, getting to his feet. "Do you need more references?"

Harvey stood also, tapping the file in front of him. "You've got good credentials, plus you have an outstanding presence. You're a strong contender." One of the dean's rare smiles surfaced. "It will be a tough decision, but the best man will win." He shook Rafiq's hand and walked him to the door. "Try to be patient."

The whole thing was starting to smell big-time. Why was this decision taking forever? He didn't have forever. If he wasn't going to get the job, then he needed to start looking elsewhere. Most schools would have already hired for the upcoming term.

Rafiq was determined not to become like Phyllis Wright, angry and complaining. Nor did he plan on hanging around Fannie Jackson, licking his wounds and feeling sorry for himself.

"You have a class to teach," Harvey said pointedly, preparing to head back into his office. "The decision should be made in a day or two."

"I'd like to believe that," Rafiq answered. Remembering Ida, who was slowly pecking away, he raised his hand in a half salute and was surprised when she deigned to grin at him. Then, practically sprinting down the hallway, he went off to teach his class of seventeen-year-olds about an era that had changed the world. It was a time when Martin Luther King Junior and Terrence Mason Senior reigned supreme and had big dreams. Both wanted equality and a fighting chance for their people.

"The prodigal daughter returns home at last," Tanya said, clinking her glass of wine against Desiree's.

Tanya was on her second glass and, as a result, this homecoming lunch was turning into a nightmare.

"Tanya," Ella said, giving her daughter a warning glare, "how about we toast to Desiree's success? She looks healthy and happy."

"How about we don't."

Ignoring her older daughter, Ella clinked her glass which held only iced tea, against Desiree's then attempted to connect with Tanya's. Her glass touched air. "We've got something to celebrate," she said, stoic as ever.

Desiree managed to produce a faint smile. She hadn't told the family she was down-and-out, with not even the promise of a job on the horizon, and she wasn't sure she was going to. They had enough to worry about.

Tanya had chosen the restaurant, in Peachtree, of course. It was patronized by an upscale group of affluent African-Americans. She sat draining the last of the wine, clearly resentful that Ella was showering Desiree with so much attention. She was used to being the star.

"So what exactly are you doing these days?" Tanya asked, her fork poised midway between plate and mouth.

"I'm teaching." The lie rolled off Desiree's tongue easily.

"My, my. What happened to those highfalutin aspirations of becoming an actress?"

Desiree flashed a wry smile. *Don't let her goad you.* "I gave those up when I decided I needed to eat."

Ella was hanging on to her every word. Desiree noticed she had barely touched her entree.

"Eat, Mother," she urged. "You mentioned you didn't have breakfast."

Ella took a dutiful stab at her fish.

"You haven't told us much about yourself," Ella said. "Are you married, divorced? Do I have more grandkids?"

Ella was asking the kinds of questions any mother would. She covered Desiree's hand with her own as Tanya pretended to be interested in the people around her.

"I'm afraid not, Mother," Desiree admitted. "I've had one or two long-term relationships but, sadly, they didn't work out."

"What's wrong with these men? Look at you. You're beautiful, well-groomed, classy and clearly intelligent. Isn't she, Tanya? We're proud of you."

Tanya's attention shifted back. She glared at both of them.

Would her mother still be proud of her if she knew she'd been fired from a prestigious prep school? If she found out how pure desperation had driven her to make a low-budget sex film, how would she react?

"Terrence Junior seems a little stressed," Desiree said, switching the subject. "I would have liked it if he could have joined us for lunch."

Tanya had called Terrence from her cell phone but he'd declined the luncheon invitation, claiming he was too busy to take the time.

"That man's always stressed," Tanya said sourly. "He's got issues."

"Stop talking about your brother like that," Ella said sternly. "He's a busy attorney with a thriving practice. He needs a woman to take care of him. I've tried fixing him up at least a half dozen times. He doesn't seem to want to marry."

Tanya snorted. "I don't think he's interested in women, Mother."

Ella looked bewildered. "Just what are you saying?" She waited for the waitress who was checking on them to leave. "Better explain yourself."

"You're in denial, Mother," Tanya huffed. "You've always been in denial. Your son is playing for the other team."

Ella rolled one of the pearls at her neck between thumb and forefinger. She still seemed not to comprehend. "Every time I've asked Terrence to join me for dinner he can't make it because he has a date."

"Sure he has dates," Tanya said, "I never said otherwise."

Desiree gave her sister a warning glance. She had gotten the picture quickly. If Tanya was on the money, the animosity between son and father was easily explained. The senior Terrence in his heyday was a macho male; he would not be able to handle or comprehend his son's choices. Desiree felt sorry for her brother. A lot of hope and money had been invested in him. Terry Junior had had the bejesus kicked out of him by a man who'd used him as validation of his virility.

Ella shifted uneasily in her seat. Desiree wasn't sure she

was that oblivious to the situation. She wondered what had caused her older sister to become such a pill? Tanya, from everything she'd heard, had the perfect marriage and an adoring husband, Ron, plus two beautiful kids. So why the attitude?

What happened to the sister she remembered—the one who'd been the annoying overachiever, perky and full of laughs? Tanya had been voted most likely to succeed by the family. Desiree had envied her most. She'd been the apple of their father's eye, while Desiree was considered the slacker. As a result, their father had directed his anger and frustration at her. She'd let him down.

What in the world had happened to turn Tanya bitter and resentful of the world?

"Anyone for dessert?" Desiree asked, hoping the energy around them would change.

"Not for me," Tanya responded, smoothing a slightly rounded stomach. "I doubt Mother would want anything, either. She's dying to return to the hospital. Aren't you Mother?"

"Yes, we should get back. Terry will be wondering where I am."

Desiree doubted the man was in any condition to wonder where anyone was. He was barely hanging on and didn't seem to have any concept of his condition. What Desiree had seen lying on that hospital bed was a shell.

"What's the prognosis, Mother?" she asked. "What's the doctor saying?"

Ella sighed wearily. "A lot of gobbly-goo. I don't think your father will ever be quite himself again. He's had a series of strokes. You see his condition."

"And they don't know when he'll be ready to leave the hospital?"

Ella sniffed. "Even if the hospital releases him, it will be to rehab. It's going to be some time before he comes home."

"So, what will you do? Hire a nurse? Winnetta, if she's still with you, must be up there in age."

The waitress was back clearing their plates. Desiree signaled for the check. The conversation resumed after she left them again.

"Your father would never allow a stranger to touch him. I guess I'll manage somehow."

Another snort came from Tanya's direction. "Don't waste your time trying to convince Ma she needs help," she said, her peevish behavior now targeted on her mother. "I've been that route—it doesn't do any good."

Desiree decided it was time to pay the check and depart. She followed her mother and sister back to the car. After this experience, dining with Terrence Junior would be a piece of cake and something to look forward to.

Already she needed a break.

CHAPTER 14

Sandi pulled into the parking lot of the French restaurant and immediately spotted Glenn Browne. He was waiting under an awning that read La Bohème. It was where they'd agreed to meet. The upscale restaurant had been his choice and Sandi, after some research, had been pleased to note its four-star rating. At least Glenn was not cheap, He was worth the manicure and facial she'd indulged in.

Sandi had been delighted with the reviews and the prices. Glenn was going all out and that said something.

He'd offered to pick her up, but Sandi had turned him down. She'd liked the idea of having her own wheels—actually, Desiree's wheels. It said she was in control of the situation and far from easy.

Sandi turned the car keys over to a waiting valet, and

stepped out. Glenn was taller than she remembered and his whole appearance shouted class, elegance and, mos important, money. She certainly could have done worse.

She hurried toward him, her stylish pumps making a click-clacking sound. Glenn was peering in the direction of the self-parking lot where he was probably expecting her to leave her car. Why would she circle a parking lot when there was someone willing to park her car for her, and for a nominal fee at that?

Sandi had been delighted to find Desiree's car in the driveway. That meant her roomie had taken a cab to the airport or called the shuttle. Either way worked to her advantage. She now had a vehicle at her disposal and it wasn't costing her a cent. Even gas would be paid for. Sandi already knew Desiree kept a credit card in the glove compartment of her car. She planned on using that card and not just for gas.

Glenn, sensing someone was almost on top of him, turned in her direction. A slow smile spread across darkly handsome features that were almost too perfect.

"You look lovely," he said, closing the distance between them.

Sandi noted his tan slacks and beautiful chocolate linen shirt. The suit jacket dangled off one finger and was positioned over his shoulder. Glenn certainly did not look like Joe Blow off the street. He radiated affluence, and the autumn colors warmed the caramel of his skin.

Shoving a handful of hair out of her eyes, Sandi tilted her cheek for his kiss.

"You look hot," she gushed, tossing him what she hoped was an encouraging smile.

"Not as hot as you."

Good boy, he knew the right things to say.

Glenn took her hand and hurried her inside the restaurant. They approached a podium where a maître d' presided. He barked orders to underlings who scurried off to do his bidding. Sandi thought he was a caricature of everything French, even up to the moustache he twirled. She suppressed a smile finding the whole scene slightly amusing.

Finally the maître d' deigned to look up.

"Monsieur Browne, good to see you." He peered over half-moon glasses at them. "You have a reservation?"

The man made it sound as if there wasn't a remote possibility of having one.

"I most certainly do," Glenn shot back, acting as if he owned the place. "My assistant spoke with someone earlier."

The reservation book was examined again.

"Ah, yes, here you are."

Sandi decided she liked Glenn's style. He didn't back down. She also considered it a good thing that he had an assistant.

One of the minions speedily led them to a table set back in a little alcove. Good, they weren't seated next to the kitchen. Sandi couldn't help noticing they were the only two African-Americans in the place. That didn't particularly bother her. She'd spent most of her adult life in Europe and that was just how it was.

A sommelier was dispatched to take their wine order. So far, and with the exception of the skeptical maître d', La Bohème had earned all of its stars. After some consultation and a brief debate on the merits of a particular merlot, Glenn ordered a bottle of wine.

"So, Sandi," Glenn asked, "What is it that you do?"

"I'm an actress."

That's all he needed to know. He didn't need to hear what kinds of films she made.

Glenn flashed a smile, one she wasn't certain how to interpret. He appeared impressed.

"I should have guessed," he said smoothly. "You are beautiful and no doubt talented, too. Have you had roles in anything I would have seen?"

Sandi tossed him what she'd been told was one of her more sultry smiles, one filled with promises of things to come. She wondered what Glenn would say if she told him that some considered her queen of the adult entertainment industry.

"That depends," she said carefully. "If you're a connoisseur of foreign films, you may have seen me in a starring role."

Glenn sat back in his chair, looking her over. His expression clearly indicated that she'd moved up a notch in his estimation.

Aware of his frank appraisal, Sandi crossed one long

leg over the other and adjusted the hem of her tight-fitting skirt. She batted mascared lashes at him and waited for the quiz that was bound to follow.

She wasn't disappointed.

"You mentioned during our conversation at the airport that you lived in Holland. What is it that brings you back to the States? And how long will you be here?"

Sandi tugged on a diamond-studded earlobe. "Well, for one, this is my home. As for how long I'm staying, that depends. I'm exhausted and need a break. Making movies can be a tiring business. I'll most likely stay for as long as it takes to feel refreshed."

"You look pretty refreshed to me," Glenn said, leaning forward and placing a hand on her knee. His hazel eyes swept over her. "Did I mention how lovely you are?"

His compliment produced another smile. "You did mention it a time or two," she said.

Sandi removed his hand from her knee and placed it back in his lap. She didn't want him thinking she was a sure thing. He needed to be kept guessing.

Glenn's expression grew remote and he placed both hands on the table. Sandi hadn't meant to rebuff him entirely. Using the tip of one finger, she lightly tapped his knuckles, bringing his attention back to her.

"What exactly is an investment banker?" she asked. "It's listed on your business card, but can you elaborate?"

"You could say I'm a financial planner. I invest large amounts of money for my wealthy clients."

Sandi uncrossed her legs, then crossed them again. Her nylons screeched and Glenn's attention shifted to her legs, as had been her intent.

"Monsieur, madame, your wine is here," the sommelier announced, intruding on their moment. He held the wine bottle, label toward them. "I think monsieur would like to sample, *oui?*"

"Madame will make the decision," Glenn answered, signaling to Sandi's glass and earning himself another point. She gave him credit for having class.

"But of course." The sommelier took a step back, opened the bottle and poured some wine into Sandi's glass. "I am confident madame will like it. It is, after all, one of our best."

The wine was then poured and Sandi dutifully sipped on it. She gave the waiter a nod of approval and when he left, Glenn raised his glass in toast to her.

"Thanks for agreeing to have dinner with me. Here's to a beautiful woman and getting to know each other."

"You're very kind."

She savored the full-bodied red, letting the liquid swirl around her tongue. It tasted like nectar, expensive and seductive. She'd caught a glimpse of the price on the wine list; it would have set most men back a paycheck or so. But Glenn didn't flinch. He was certainly making an effort to impress her.

"You haven't even glanced at the menu," Glenn reminded, nudging the bill of fare toward her. "Let me make a few suggestions, if I may."

"Please do. I'll defer to your good judgment."

"Thank you. Although you wouldn't think so from the maître d's greeting, I come here often. Phillipe is a snotty piece of work and much too full of himself."

After flipping open the menu, Glenn pointed at several choices. "The escargot is excellent for starters. It's made in a wonderful wine sauce. If you choose the veal as the main course you won't be disappointed. Then, of course, there is the fish. Salmon served with mushrooms and capers is a favorite of mine. It's à la carte, so be sure to order a vegetable and starch."

The choices sounded delicious and she was hungry.

"What are you going to have?" she asked.

"A Caesar salad to start and I am partial to a good cut of beef."

"I'll go with the seafood, then. The shrimp and scallop dish is very tempting.

"Not only tempting but delicious. And while you are making your choices I shall feast my eyes on you."

Glenn was certainly laying on the charm. She loved it. It felt nice to be appreciated and wanted. She wasn't getting any younger and it felt good to know she still had it.

She closed her menu and took a slow sip of wine. Sensing they were ready, a waitress appeared.

Glenn, clearly in charge, consulted with her before placing their orders.

"Where's your friend this evening?" he asked when the waitress disappeared.

Sandi frowned, "Which friend?"

"The one who picked you up at the airport."

Why did he care? "You mean Desiree?" She tossed him a quizzical look.

"Beautiful name. Is she as beautiful to live with?" Sandi decided to be careful. She wasn't quite sure why he was so interested in Desiree.

"Desiree is visiting her folks in Atlanta. Where is your family from, Glenn?"

What she really meant to ask was if he was married. She hadn't noticed a ring on his left finger or an untanned spot where that ring might have been. Even so, Sandi's intuition told her that he was involved.

"What remains of my family lives in Indianapolis," he said. "What about you? Where is your family from?"

"New Jersey. I'm divorced."

She'd given him an opening, but he didn't bite. Not that it mattered to her whether he was attached or not. She'd gone that route before. Although it wasn't pleasant, she'd made it work. But it would be far less complicated if there wasn't a wife in the picture.

Using the tip of a Prada pump, Sandi nudged Glenn's shoe-clad instep. He tapped back with the toe of an equally expensive loafer. There they were, two grown people playing footsies under the table.

It was time to turn up the heat a bit and see where this led. Sandi leaned across the table assaulting Glenn with a view of her more than ample cleavage.

He was gentleman enough not to openly gape although she could tell he wanted to.

"Fortune smiled on me when I ran into you at the airport," Glenn said, again sipping on his wine.

"Fortune smiled on both of us."

Glenn reached across the table and took her hand. "You are lovely and intelligent—everything I have been looking for in a lady."

What a line of BS.

Fortunately their waitress returned, saving her from answering.

"Your first course is here," she chirped, disturbing what could very well have been an intimate moment. "Your salad, sir, and the lady ordered the crawfish Louisiana-style."

From then on, dinner seemed to take forever, but it did give them time to talk about many things. Sandi discovered that Glenn stayed at an executive hotel when he was in town. The bank's headquarters was actually in Manhattan. He claimed to own a number of investment properties all over the country. After some skillful questioning, Sandi learned that he had one child from a previous marriage. That was another plus in his favor as far as she was concerned.

When asked if she wanted dessert, Sandi declined but settled for cappuccino. Glenn kept her company while sipping on espresso.

Finally, the bill was presented, signaling their time together had ended—or maybe it had just begun.

"What do you think?" Glenn asked. "Shall we find ourselves a hole-in-the-wall jazz club or shall we call it a night?"

Sandi pretended to give it some consideration. The seconds dragged by.

"I'd like to see your place," she said boldly. "Surely you have some jazz CDs, and room service could provide us a nice bottle of wine. If we pass on the club would that be a good compromise?"

"Compromise, hell. From the moment I laid eyes on you, I've wanted to take you home with me."

All of a sudden Glenn's efforts to be blasé were thrown to the wind. He laced his fingers through hers. "I've wanted to get to know you better from the moment I met you."

She'd bet. There was no mistaking what he was after. A fool she wasn't.

Sandi picked up her purse.

"I'll get my car from the valet and follow you."

Glenn's eyebrows rose. "Aren't we riding together?"

Did she look that stupid? No one she knew of went to a stranger's place without having some means of escape at hand.

She stroked Glenn's arm through the expensive cotton shirt. "How am I going to get home if I leave my vehicle here? The restaurant will probably be closed when I leave your place. The valet will have my car impounded."

"Good point. You'll follow me, then?"

"I will."

Glenn took her parking ticket from her and they hurriedly exited the restaurant.

So far things were turning out even better than she'd planned.

CHAPTER 15

"I wish I could make out what he was saying," Ella said, her arm circling Desiree's shoulder as they stared down at the still figure in the hospital bed.

"Mother, my guess is he's probably having a hard time breathing and he's gasping for air. Look at him. He's not exactly lucid."

A loud snort followed then Ella said, "Good Lord, child, when did you become so cynical? If you don't hope, you have nothing."

Hope was something Desiree had plenty of. She had to. And she wouldn't exactly call herself cynical either, just not emotionally invested. Emotions kept her from thinking clearly. Emotions got in the way.

Desiree took a step back from the hospital bed, quietly

contemplating it all. Her mother must be totally delusional. The smell of death and decay lingered in the air. It was only a matter of time before Terrence Senior left them.

Desiree's packed bag sat next to the hospital door so she could make a quick exit. Her brother had agreed to drive her to the airport; he should be here in minutes. Desiree had wanted to grab a cab, but Terrence Junior would not hear of it. Despite his busy schedule, he'd actually insisted he drive her to the airport himself.

It might have something to do with their dinner last evening. Although it had not been the relaxing event Desiree had hoped for, they'd somehow found common ground. In the two hours spent together they'd bonded in a strange way.

Terrence had even managed to let his hair down a bit. He'd confided that self-preservation was his reason for putting distance between himself and the family. He confessed he found the family totally dysfunctional.

He'd shared his memories of growing up hearing his mother's anguished screams as she pleaded with their father not to hurt her. He'd overheard the loud arguments, the accusations of infidelity. And how could he not? The fights had gone on and on into the wee hours of the morning. Even earplugs had been useless.

And over dessert, a tasty tiramisu, Terrence had freely admitted to hating his father. He could not and would not forgive the transgressions of the man who had kept him quaking most of his childhood and wetting his bed until he was almost a teenager. The memories of the beatings he'd gotten and those he'd witnessed were still vivid in his mind. He resented his mother for putting up with the old man's vile behavior. And now he just wished the old man was dead.

Those would have been Desiree's exact sentiments up until a few days ago. Before she'd seen the skeleton of the man who no longer resembled the virile Dr. Mason. Now she pitied Terrence Mason and couldn't help wondering why he'd gone bad.

Her mother was a trusting soul who'd fallen in love with a charismatic man. And she had cast her lot with him. Desiree wondered how long it had taken her to discover he had little respect for women. Having experienced what she had as a child, Desiree had vowed to remain single rather than put up with abuse of any kind, verbal or physical.

Enough of this visit down memory lane. She'd done what she'd come to do. It was time to head home. This was as good as it was going to get with the Mason family. But at least they were talking. They'd made an effort to put aside the past. More important, Desiree had made peace with herself.

Going home to Bethesda was beginning to look better and better. All this drama could wear a person down. Her life was really a piece of cake compared to her mother's.

"I have to go, Mother," Desiree said, disentangling herself from Ella's embrace. "I don't want to miss my plane, and Terrence Junior must be waiting."

Ella heaved out a watery sigh. "You'd think that boy would come up and get you. Who would believe I raised a child with such poor manners?"

"Poor manners has nothing to do with it. Terrence is just busy," Desiree said covering for her brother. "It's nice of him to drive me to the airport."

"It would be nicer if he made time to see his father."

What was the use? Ella chose not to understand. There was no point even addressing that issue. Ella was in denial. She just did not want to believe that Terrence Junior wanted nothing to do with his father and had no intention of coming around. Desiree had no intention of bursting her bubble.

"I really do have to go, Mother," Desiree said, kissing her mother's rouged cheek. "If something uh...happens to him," she looked over at her father, "call me and I'll come back."

Ella choked back a sob. "Nothing's going to happen to your father. It can't. He wouldn't just abandon me. I've missed you, baby," she said to Desiree, holding on to her as if she were an anchor. "You have no idea just how much."

Desiree inhaled what smelled like a full bottle of Chanel. Ella's embrace was suffocating. Finally, she managed to disentangle herself. She gave a quick glance at the bed. Determined to put the past aside, she laid a hand on the emaciated limb shrouded by starched white sheets.

An almost discernible flutter occurred. Terrence Senior's good eye shot open and a wheeze came from the base of his throat. Spittle trickled. Desiree averted her eyes. She inwardly chastised herself for thinking him grotesque.

"See," Ella said in a reverent whisper, "I told you your father knew you were here. He doesn't respond like this when Tanya comes to visit."

Terrence Senior probably sensed her grudging presence and felt the hostility in the air, Desiree thought irreverently.

"Tell Tanya I'll be in touch. She's got my cell as well as my home number now."

Desiree forced herself to squeeze her father's arm.

"I'll say a prayer for you," she said. "I hope you have a swift recovery."

Desiree doubted he would. The man was almost dead. Sheer willpower was what kept him alive now. She gave her mother a quick hug, grabbed her bag and hurried from the room.

As she approached the lobby, Desiree realized she was crying. There was a lump in her throat the size of an ostrich egg. She needed to pull herself together.

She'd come home and done what any decent daughter would do. Now it was back to reality. The next time she returned to Atlanta, Terrence Mason Senior would most likely be dead.

Rafiq had called Desiree's house and gotten Sandi. She told him that Desiree was back in town. To date, she still had not called him and he wondered what that was about. He'd thought they'd had a great time and he'd been pleasantly surprised to discover the attraction between them was mutual. If he did not hear from her by tonight he planned on calling her.

With only a few weeks left to the school term, a decision had to been made soon about Harvey's replacement, if it hadn't been made already.

On the way to his next class, Rafiq spotted Phyllis Wright heading toward him. Just what he needed. The woman was a downer and her negativity was a blight. He managed to smile at her anyway.

"Hi, Phyllis."

"Hey, Rafiq, how's it going? Have you heard anything about who Harvey chose?"

"Not a word, Phyllis."

She snorted loudly, a most unladylike sound. "Maybe you need to keep your ear to the ground. Rumor has it Harvey's already picked his replacement."

"Really? If that's the case, no one's informed me."

Rafiq couldn't tell whether there was credence to her words or whether she was deliberately baiting him.

Phyllis stepped closer as if eager to spread her cancer.

"You might as well know since you'll find out soon enough—the board's chosen Conrad Maloney, the outside candidate. Big surprise, huh? It's just plain nepotism, if you ask me."

Rafiq tried to keep his expression neutral as though he

wasn't at all surprised by Phyllis's revelation, if what she'd just said was true. He'd expected something like this, but had hoped his credentials would speak for themselves. Even so, the news should have come from Harvey and not this bitchy woman with an obvious ax to grind.

"Where did you hear this, Phyllis?" Rafiq asked carefully.

"Oh, I have my ways. I kinda knew this was how it would play out. Blood wins out usually."

Much as he hated gossip, Rafiq wished he had the time to question Phyllis further, but he didn't. A classroom of rambunctious teenagers awaited.

What he'd do is pay a surprise visit to Harvey Coleman later. He didn't particularly appreciate hearing about this from Phyllis. Of course, the witch might simply be blowing hot air. She, after all, had been disqualified early in the process.

"How about we catch up later?" Rafiq said. "I'll stop by the teachers' lounge after class and maybe we can have a cup of coffee together."

"Sounds like a plan."

With that, Phyllis waddled off and Rafiq continued on in the opposite direction.

The next hour went by relatively quickly. Rafiq gave the class a quiz and used the time to make notes for a new chapter of the book. His mind was not fully on the classroom of hyperactive teens reluctantly taking a multiple-choice test. His thoughts were on what he would say to

Harvey Coleman and what to do with his life. If what Phyllis said was true and he was not Harvey's successor, he'd definitely have to make some plans.

"Okay, that's it. Pencils down. Start passing your quizzes to the end of the row," Rafiq announced. "Dina, will you please collect the tests and bring them to me?

Dina, a slightly overweight junior, was only too happy to be thrown into the spotlight. She rose to do his bidding. There were groans mixed with sighs of relief, but finally every last test was collected and Rafiq dismissed the class.

He headed off to see Harvey. Usually an appointment was necessary, but in this case he wanted the element of surprise to be on his side.

The moment he entered the outer office, Rafiq spotted Ida perusing some papers. She must have heard him, because her head popped up and she squinted over wire-framed spectacles.

"Good afternoon, Rafiq. Do you have an appointment with Harvey?"

"No, Ida. I was hoping that perhaps he could spare ten minutes of his time to see me. Something rather urgent has come up."

"Well, I don't know. Mr. Coleman's a busy person." She glanced at Rafiq again. Perhaps it was something in his expression that made her add, "Let me see if he can fit you in."

After an extended conversation behind closed doors, Ida returned.

"Harvey has another meeting in five minutes, but he said he could see you now. If you'll make it quick."

Rafiq thanked her before heading off to The Rack.

Harvey was standing at the window looking down on the rolling green lawns as if he owned the place. He didn't turn around, although he knew Rafiq was there.

"Jones, I'm afraid we'll have to make this quick. I've got a meeting with one of the board members off campus."

"Thank you for seeing me on such short notice," Rafiq said, positioning himself in front of the desk.

This time Harvey deigned to turn around. "Ida mentioned it was urgent," he said. "She said you seemed a little stressed. What is it that I can do for you?"

What was it he could do for him? Come on, the man should know. There was less than a week left to the school term and Harvey had to know he needed to hear something.

"I'm here to confirm a rumor," Rafiq said, his eyes never leaving Harvey's face.

Harvey's fingers fastened around one mother of pearl cuff link. "And what would that rumor be?"

"It seems to be public knowledge that you've made a decision. I've not been notified."

Harvey's expression was totally guarded now. "Where did you hear that?"

The exchange was getting absurd. It seemed to be going around in circles. Harvey was clearly hedging. Rafiq no longer had patience for this.

"Let's just say I heard that Conrad Maloney was told he had the position. If that's the case, doesn't professional courtesy dictate I be notified? I'm a little irritated that I had to hear this on the street."

"How do these things get out?" Harvey said as if speaking to himself. Turning, he took long strides, seeking refuge behind the barrier that was his desk.

Rafiq felt as if he'd had the wind knocked out of him. It was one thing to hear what he'd hoped was speculation from Phyllis Wright, and another to hear it from the man who was allegedly the decision maker. It wasn't a particularly good feeling to know he was no longer in the running, if he'd ever been. But at least now he could make some definite plans.

Going through the motions, Rafiq stuck out his hand. "Thanks for the opportunity, Harvey. I guess I should be grateful to have gotten this far."

Harvey now stood. He looked visibly relieved that Rafiq had taken the news calmly.

"You were definitely a contender, always have been. Look at the job you did here at Fannie Jackson. I've had a couple of resignations, so I am certain I can find you something."

How cavalier of Harvey and, in some ways, how utterly insulting! Harvey thought that tossing him a bone would make him happy. He expected him to roll over on his back with all fours in the air, panting. He could find him something, indeed. Hell no, he had his pride.

Rafiq forced a smile and told an outright lie. "Not at all necessary, Harvey. I was offered another position, which I put on hold awaiting the outcome of this one. It's safe to say I won't be returning to Fannie Jackson in the fall."

Harvey actually looked disappointed. "I'm sorry to hear that. You were an asset to the faculty."

That backhanded compliment did nothing for him. It did not make up for a job that should have been his. Instead, Harvey had hired an outsider.

Gathering what was left of his dignity, Rafiq left.

CHAPTER 16

"Desiree, this is Conrad Maloney. How are you, girl?"

Desiree's guard instantly went up. It was going on five weeks since she'd lost her job, and this was the first she'd heard from him. Conrad had turned out to be some friend.

"Managing, Conrad. Managing. I'm on my way out for a run. Was there something you wanted?"

A fairly lengthy pause followed. Conrad was no fool. He had probably picked up on her coolness.

"Why don't you give me a call when you get done?" he said before disconnecting.

Something most definitely was up. Why now, out of the blue, did Conrad feel the need to reconnect? She'd go for a run and then satisfy her curiosity later.

Desiree had been running for almost an hour before she slowed down. Her breath was coming in raspy little bursts and in another ten minutes euphoria would set in.

Pumping her arms, she willed her legs to continue moving. She ignored the tightness in her chest, knowing that this, too, would pass once she got beyond a certain stage. Getting out and running had been a good decision. It helped clear her head. She was still on sensory overload after her visit to Atlanta and needed to calm down.

Desiree had been overjoyed not to find Sandi home when she'd gotten back. But she'd not been at all happy to find her house a mess, with clothing strewn everywhere and dishes piled in the sink. Her car had also been gone from the driveway. She needed to have a serious discussion with Sandi that could no longer be put off.

A quarter of a mile later, Desiree decided to give it up. As she limped home she visualized a steaming-hot shower. She would call Rafiq and then Conrad after she was done.

During her run, Desiree had decided she would tell Rafiq she would work for him. The job came with a salary, and getting up and out every day would provide some much-needed structure to her life. At the very least, it was a temporary fix until she found a real job.

Desiree jogged in place in front of the town house before stretching out. Beads of sweat trickled down her face and in between her breasts. But despite being hot and sweaty, she felt energized.

Desiree's empty driveway was a reminder that she needed to assert herself and to heck with the consequences. She'd been lugging around baggage for far too long. Who would really care about something that had happened ages ago? Sandi had pushed their friendship to the limit.

A car horn tooted behind her. Desiree got out of the way seconds before Sandi shot into her reserved parking spot.

"Hey, you're back," she said through the open passenger window, making Desiree feel as if she was the visitor and not the home owner. "I've been running errands. I didn't think you would mind me taking your car."

"It would have been nice of you to ask," Desiree mumbled as Sandi hopped out of the vehicle.

"You weren't around to ask," Sandi calmly answered. "I figured since you left your keys visible you expected me to drive your car."

The direct approach seemed the best way to go. Desiree obviously wasn't getting through. "Perhaps we should talk about you renting a car," she said, taking the bull by the horns.

"Why?" Sandi asked, genuinely puzzled. She popped her sunglasses on her head and wrinkled her nose. "Why would I need a rental? It's not like you're working. Having two cars here would be a waste of time."

She headed up the walkway, leaving Desiree to follow.

Inside the house, Desiree said through gritted teeth, "I'm going to take a shower. When I get out we'll talk some more."

"Can it hold until tomorrow?" Sandi countered. "I'm running late and I have dinner plans." She stalked into the bedroom.

When Desiree got out of the shower, Sandi was on the phone; her words were interspersed with peals of laughter. Despite that, Desiree caught snippets of the conversation. Sandi was firming up dinner plans with a man. It occurred to Desiree that the man could be Byron. That made her angry.

"So you'll pick me up in fifteen minutes?" Sandi said. "I'll be ready to go."

And although Desiree couldn't care less what her ex did, Sandi's blatant disrespect for her rankled. As soon as she hung up, Desiree asked nonchalantly, "Was that anyone I know?"

"Actually, yes, Glenn Browne, the man I was talking to at the airport. Do you have an evening purse I can borrow?"

The woman's boldness annoyed Desiree, but what was the point in being petty?

"I'm sure there's something in my closet to complement that outfit."

She hiked an eyebrow, taking in the tight-fitting copper-colored dress. The shade complemented Sandi's cinnamon skin. The actress wore stiletto heels, and chandelier earrings skimmed her shoulders.

"What about that brass purse with the chain-link handle?" Sandi suggested as if she were entitled.

"I'll get it for you," Desiree said, going to find the purse. It was better than having Sandi rifle through her things. Who knew what else she would want to borrow?

When Desiree returned to the living room, Sandi had a bright red cashmere shawl draped over one shoulder and looked every inch the movie star. Desiree handed her the purse and, without thanking her, Sandi emptied the contents of her hobo bag on the coffee table. She began transferring lipstick, wallet, compact and a square foil package that must be a condom. She was obviously planning a busy night.

"We'll talk at breakfast," Desiree proposed.

"I may not be back."

Sandi winked at her. At that inopportune time the doorbell rang.

"My date is here," Sandi announced. "I wouldn't wait up if I were you." She went off to answer the door.

Glenn Browne was not asked in. Desiree waited until the door closed firmly behind them before pouring a glass of wine. She picked up the phone and punched in Rafiq's number. He answered on the third ring.

"Desiree," he said, having probably checked his caller ID. "When did you get back?"

"A few days ago."

"So how did it go?"

Rafiq's tone was warm, friendly and encouraging. It actually warmed her. She was glad to hear his voice.

"As well as these things ever go," Desiree answered

carefully. She desperately needed a friend, someone who was not judgmental and would listen, someone who didn't want to use her.

"Oh, this doesn't sound good. Want to talk about it?"

"I'm not sure you'd understand," Desiree said, coming to a sudden decision. "Have you eaten? If not, what say we meet at Senor Grogg's? I'll fill you in there."

"I would love to meet you at the restaurant but I've just ordered in ribs and potato salad." A pause followed. "Can I tempt you? There's plenty for two."

Desiree wondered if his offer was prompted by a desire to pick up where they'd left off. Just in case, she'd better set him straight. Much as she was attracted to him, agreeing to come over wasn't an invitation to take her to bed.

"Okay," Desiree agreed. "We could discuss my job description—that is if you're still interested in having me work for you."

Rafiq's tone rose a notch. "Does that mean you've made up your mind?"

"We'll iron out the details when I get there. Give me directions to your place."

After Rafiq had walked her through getting to his home, Desiree punched in Conrad's number. The phone rang for what seemed forever and eventually the machine picked up. Desiree left her name and number before hanging up.

She glanced in the bathroom mirror and decided the stylish tracksuit she had on would have to do. After adding a touch of makeup, she headed out the door. Fifteen minutes later, she pulled up in front of Rafiq's rented house.

A redwood fence circled the ranch-style home set back from the road. Through the open car window, Desiree inhaled the scent of a freshly mowed lawn. Climbing out of her vehicle, she approached the latched gate. The view before her was spectacular.

An arbor covered in trailing vines stood off to the side. A koi pond contained a number of lethargic fish swimming sluggishly among lily pads. Desiree opened the gate and walked up a path edged by red and white impatiens. She stopped in front of Rafiq's door, took a deep breath and rang the bell.

The door flew open immediately. Rafiq, dressed in jeans and a sweatshirt, greeted her with a kiss.

"How were my directions?" he asked.

"Perfect," Desiree said, following him in.

The living room matched the outdoors. Tasteful. It had the requisite sofa and coffee table. A tremendous mahogany étagère held a television set and many books. The polished wooden floors sported an assortment of Persian rugs. Ferns hung from the vaulted ceilings.

The effect was masculine yet eclectic at the same time. The étagère, Desiree guessed, was possibly an antique. Rafiq Jones was a man of surprises. Presuming the furniture was his, he had style.

The dining room where they eventually ended up held

an oval oak table where two places were set. The room also had a fireplace that remained unlit.

"Our food arrived just minutes ago," Rafiq said, holding out a chair for Desiree. "Let's eat before dinner gets cold."

They were halfway through the meal, the conversation centering on Desiree's trip to Atlanta, when the tears began to spill. Rafiq covered her hand with his.

"Just let it out. It had to be tough seeing your family after all this time. But at least you made the effort. It sounds like you bonded with your mother and brother."

"Yes, in a strange way I did. I realized how dysfunctional my family really is. My mother lives in this fantasy world, and my brother, well, he's just plain angry and refuses to interact."

"What about your sister? You mentioned she has a family of her own."

"Yes, but she tends to play the martyr and she's resentful of me and of the time she commits to my mother and father. Enough of me. What about you? Have you heard anything about the dean's position?"

Rafiq put his knife and fork aside. He took a sip of water. "Yes, as a matter of fact I have. Harvey decided to go with Conrad Maloney."

Desiree felt as if she'd been punched in the chest. What a son of a bitch.

"That's too bad," she said evenly. "But it does explain something."

It explained what a snake Conrad Maloney was. That was why he'd called, of course, to gloat or pick her brain. He had to know she would hear he'd gotten the job.

"What does it explain?"

"Why Conrad called me."

"What did he want?"

Desiree explained they'd only spoken briefly.

"And you've known this guy for how long?" Rafiq asked.

"For as long as I've worked for Fannie Jackson. Conrad is qualified for the position, but I never thought of him as being particularly ambitious. I guess I was wrong. This changes everything for you. Doesn't it?"

Rafiq, who now appeared deep in thought, chewed on his food before swallowing. "Yes, it does. I'll have to look for another job and most probably will relocate." He pushed his plate aside. "I'm done."

Perhaps Zinga had been wrong about him after all, and perhaps Desiree had been wrong to suspect his motives. If Rafiq had conspired against her, it had been to no avail; getting her fired hadn't benefited him in the least.

"I'm sorry you didn't get the job," Desiree said, meaning it. She stood and began gathering their dishes. "I'll help you clean up. Then we can talk about your book."

Rafiq's eyes lit up. Desiree could tell that this project consumed his waking hours. Together they worked to clear the table and stash the dirty dinnerware in the dishwasher. While coffee was perking they chatted about one thing or another. And, finally, mugs in hand, they retired to the living room.

"Here are my notes," Rafiq said, once they got settled. He handed over a couple of folders. "I need to get them organized and I need to print out what I've done so far on the manuscript. Read it through, keeping in mind sentence structure, and flow, then give me feedback."

"Is there a specific publishing house you've targeted?" Desiree asked. "What about an agent?"

"I've tried querying agents. I've had a couple of bites, but nothing definite."

"Yes, I've heard it's tough to find representation. We should send out letters every day or so. What is it that makes your book unique?"

Rafiq thought for a moment. "Most books addressing the topic of bipolar syndrome are cut-and-dried. There's an almost clinical approach to sharing information about the disease. I'm trying to humanize the facts and explain there's no shame in having a mental illness. This book is about helpful coping mechanisms. If the disorder is diagnosed early and the patient receives the right medication, families with a bipolar relative can live pretty normal lives. They just have to pay attention to certain behaviors and recognize when there's a problem."

"What you're doing is admirable and tough," Desiree said, meaning it. "It must be so painful to write about your experience. Every time you put pen to paper, you have to be reliving every aching moment of your loss. Losing a child is never easy."

Rafiq's expression grew serious. His jaw muscle worked. "You speak as if from experience," he said. "And that's the second time you've said this. But you've never been married. You have no children."

"Some things you just know instinctively," Desiree said, hugging her secret to her. She wasn't quite ready to share it with him.

Rafiq continued as if talking to himself, "This project is therapy for me. Even if the book never gets published, it will help me work through a slew of issues."

There was pain and suffering on his face and, along with that, something else. Determination. Rafiq had gotten over the tragedy of death and divorce and was coping as best as he could. She had to admire his fortitude and tremendous courage.

Were the roles reversed, and if she'd kept her child, how would she have coped if her daughter had been diagnosed with a mental illness? Would her sanity have remained intact if her child had taken her life? And would she now have the courage to write about it, exposing her pain to the world? Desiree doubted it.

Interacting with teenagers everyday had to be challenging and painful for Rafiq. It had to be a constant reminder of the loss he'd suffered. Yet, instead of bemoaning his lot in life, he was doing something useful and meaningful. He was documenting the painful moments and sharing his experiences so that others could learn.

Rafiq deserved to be published.

"On another note," he said, changing the topic, "your friend Sandi's been calling me."

"Why?"

Rafiq shrugged. "Who knows? She goes on about one thing or another. Once it was about some kind of bug that had gotten into the house. Another time your car engine was making a knocking sound."

Desiree's eyebrows shot skyward. "She was angling for you to come over, right?"

"I suppose. I told her I was busy. How long is she staying, anyway?"

"As long as it takes to pack her things," Desiree said, coming to an immediate decision.

This was simply the last straw. Sandi had moved into her home and taken up residence. It was one thing for her to borrow Desiree's things and disrupt her orderly life, another to move in on any man who paid Desiree attention. Friends like that were not worth keeping. She'd end the free ride, and the consequences be damned.

It was worth taking a chance. There was nothing else to lose.

CHAPTER 17

"Oh, baby, baby! You make me feel so good."

Glenn was in the throes of an orgasm and, though Sandi knew his words were bed talk, they did make her feel like the most desirable woman in the world. She needed that kind of affirmation badly, especially after what she'd been through. She'd been fired from her latest flick and dumped by the guy she used for recreational sex.

Sandi tightened her thighs around Glenn's and gyrated. Glenn's face was contorted and his ejaculation came in short, quick bursts. His juices poured into her and when he was spent, she relaxed her muscles.

She'd already gotten hers—multiple times. She was now relaxed and feeling as if she could take on the world.

Seconds later Glenn was asleep and snoring. Sandi slid out from under his muscular body and padded barefoot across the industrial hotel carpeting. She retrieved her purse and headed for the bathroom to clean up and check the messages on her cell phone.

After accessing her voice mail, she retrieved her messages. Quite a number of them except the one she'd hoped for. Rafiq Jones still hadn't called. But there was one from Byron wanting to get together. She'd return that call in a day or two when she got around to it. Give him a taste of his own medicine lest he take her for granted.

Sandi stepped into the shower and turned on the faucet. She let the hot water drench her satiated body before using the washcloth to lather up and scrub the residue left from lovemaking. Glenn seemed an interesting man but she suspected he was married. She couldn't seem to get much information out of him.

Yes, she had major reservations but she still planned on sticking around. There wasn't anything better on the horizon. And he had bought her a beautiful gold bracelet. That said he wasn't cheap.

"Where are you, babe?" His deep voice came from the outer room.

"Taking a shower."

"I'll be right in."

That was another thing she liked about him—no pussyfooting around. He was clear about what he wanted.

He shoved the shower curtain aside and stepped in. He palmed the washcloth and began soaping her body. Glenn's mouth fastened on one nipple. He used the washcloth to caress her in the most intimate of places.

Sandi savored the heat of the shower. She closed her eyes and inhaled the perfumed lather all the while sliding her hands down Glenn's rib cage and settling them on his burgeoning erection.

"I like," she said.

"Me, too, babe, but I'm heading to New York tomorrow. I'll need to get some sleep. Rain check for later this week, then? I'll call and set something up."

"That would be nice. Are you leaving me a number where I can reach you?" Sandi asked.

Glenn nibbled on her earlobe. "You've got my cell, babe. That's all you need."

He was being evasive, again confirming what she believed. There must be a wife in the picture.

"So when will you be back?" Sandi asked. "I'd like to make plans for the weekend."

"No one's stopping you."

It wasn't what she wanted to hear.

Glenn slid a hand over her mouth and the other between her thighs and Sandi forgot all about getting annoyed. She gyrated against his open palm. Glenn backed her up against the tile wall and settled his growing erection against her core.

"Love me, baby," Sandi invited, spreading her legs wide.

Glenn, needing no further urging, did just that.

* * *

Zinga had accompanied Desiree to the Chesapeake area and now they were making their way home. Desiree had done a mass mailing of résumés and actually had several bites; one of them came from a small, practically all-white private school advertising for a principal. She'd been delighted when the school secretary called to say the current principal wanted to see her.

Zinga, good friend that she was, had insisted on accompanying Desiree on the long drive. Now that school was out, she had plenty of time on her hands. While Desiree had her interviews, Zinga went shopping.

Desiree had met with a succession of faculty members. Overall, the interviews seemed to go well. But Desiree refused to make too much of it. Her first interview had been with the current principal, an ageing woman with a face that could strip primer off a wall. At the conclusion of their talk she'd said she would be speaking with Harvey Coleman. Desiree wasn't sure she could count on Harvey not to say anything about why she left Fannie Jackson. He was such a principled man and could easily let it slip her departure hadn't been of her own volition.

Oh, well, she could only hope that Harvey would be circumspect.

"Oldie or not, I just love this song," Zinga practically screamed, turning up the radio a notch and providing off-key backup to a Smoky Robinson tune.

Desiree smiled over at her friend. "Yes, those were the days. My mother used to have these old records and my sister and I would dance with her. We had all the moves down pat."

Using her arms, Desiree began mimicking the old synchronized movements of The Platters.

Zinga just giggled. "Ah, girlfriend, you're almost back. Life will get better, I promise."

"Life has already gotten better. Today I had an interview."

She'd decided better to be optimistic and think positive thoughts.

"So how did the interview go? You really haven't said much. But you do seem pretty upbeat."

"It went well, I think," Desiree answered carefully. "Hopefully, I'll get another interview soon. I need to find something before summer ends. There's only so far my savings will go."

Zinga patted her thigh. "Someone will scoop you up, girl. You'll have your pick. Any school should be salivating to have you. You've got a good track record."

"A lot of good that did me. I still got fired."

Desiree stared up at the setting sun. Zinga had put the top of her Mustang convertible down; and a tangy breeze ruffled her dreads. It caused wisps of Desiree's hair to escape the severe bun she'd pulled her hair back into for the interview. But she didn't care. It had been a long time since she'd felt this relaxed and hopeful.

"Have you heard from Conrad again?" Zinga asked, taking a turn in the road at an alarmingly high speed that was well over the limit.

"No. He never returned my call."

"That's not a surprise. He was probably just trying to feel you out."

Desiree glanced over at her friend again. "Why would he do that?"

"Because I'm beginning to think he's the snake. Maybe I was wrong about Rafiq after all. He got passed over, too, and he did offer you a job. How's that going?"

It was too early to tell, although Rafiq seemed pleased.

"I've only been over to his place a couple of times," Desiree said. "I've gotten his notes in order. He leaves me the key under the front mat. I think he's been job hunting. He keeps going out of town."

Zinga scrunched up her nose. "I'm surprised, because I heard Harvey offered him a full-time position. I thought he would have grabbed it. Miranda Woods is taking early retirement. Her husband was offered a job up north and she's packing up her house and kids."

Desiree angled her face upward to catch what remained of the sun. "I wonder why Rafiq hasn't mentioned it? He's pretty soured on Harvey, though, and I'm not sure he's been that happy at Fannie Jackson."

Rafiq hadn't been that forthcoming about his personal life. What little she knew resulted from reading his notes. There'd been no repeat of their interlude. Desiree had decided he'd lost interest in her, while she, however, was growing more interested in him.

"Rafiq has every reason to be soured," Zinga said, her dreads whipping against her cheeks. "He's probably heard the same rumors I have."

"What rumors?"

"You don't know? Rafiq hasn't told you? " She glanced over at Desiree again, her expression incredulous. "Phyllis found out that Conrad Maloney's related to Harvey's wife. No wonder he got the job."

"What? I can't believe you would both keep this from me." Desiree turned off the radio.

Zinga's eyes left the road for an instant. She met Desiree's gaze head-on. "I've known for weeks. I didn't want to upset you. Phyllis Wright was the one who found out. Of course, initially no one paid Phyllis much mind. She does like to gossip. Everyone figured she was just bitter and looking to stir up stuff. But then Ida let it slip in a conversation with Freda Owens, who teaches home economics. You remember her, right? She and Freda are friends. And Freda, of course, couldn't wait to share the news with the rest of us."

Desiree's fingers drummed against the dashboard. The more she thought about it, the more it made sense. Why would Harvey choose an outsider over highly qualified faculty members? Maybe Conrad was the one to send Harvey that tape. He could have perceived her as a threat. But how would he have found out about an X-rated film that had never even been released? She didn't recall telling him about her adventures as an actress. But during their long lunches they'd talked about a number of things, so anything was possible.

"I'm pissed off," Desiree admitted aloud. "Blood always wins out. None of us ever stood a chance."

"Umm-hmm. And you know what I'm thinking? That Conrad is a real snake in the grass, befriending you, then falling off the face of the earth when it was convenient."

"You know what?" Desiree said, a thought popping into her head. "I'll give Conrad a call tonight and extend my congratulations. Let's see how he reacts."

They'd exited the highway and were now heading toward Desiree's home. Zinga remained quiet, a sure indication that something was cooking in that highly active brain.

"I wonder," she said after a while, "what Conrad would say if you confronted him about being related to Harvey's wife? Bet you he would start sputtering."

"Conrad never sputters. He's cool, calm, collected and very eloquent. But you're onto something. I will give him a call. I won't mention a word about him disappearing. I'll pretend I need his advice and invite him to lunch. Let's see what he says to that."

Zinga snorted, then beamed. Desiree sensed her imagination had gone wild. They were now in Desiree's complex and Zinga's lead foot eased up. A good thing, too, because children were skateboarding in the middle of the narrow streets and after-work joggers were out in full force.

On Desiree's block, Zinga slowed down the car even more.

"Is that woman still staying with you?" she asked as she slid into Desiree's reserved spot.

"That woman as in Sandi?"

"When is she leaving?"

Desiree groaned, simultaneously rolling her eyes. "Who knows? I've been trying to set up time for a talk, but she's been avoiding me."

"Do it soon," Zinga urged, parking the car. "She's another snake you have to watch. I saw her at Senor Grogg's the other night hanging all over Byron. I didn't let her see me. The way they were carrying on, they really needed to get a room." Zinga snorted in disgust.

Desiree's hand was already on the door handle. She paused. "Are you sure you saw them? I could swear Sandi and Byron were a one-time thing. He hasn't called her that I know of. She's been seeing some guy she met at the airport."

"There's nothing wrong with my eyesight," Zinga said. "The witch is probably playing them both. Not that they don't deserve it. Men! Besides, you wouldn't know if Byron's been calling. Sandi has a cell phone. Speaking of which, isn't that her pulling up in a rental car?"

Sure enough, Sandi was parking the car she'd been forced to rent after Desiree put her foot down. She got out and approached the Mustang, motioning for Desiree to open the window.

"I wondered where you'd gone to," Sandi said, eyeing Desiree's business suit. "Did you have an interview? How did it go?"

"We'll talk later," Desiree said, and quickly made the introductions.

Zinga bared her teeth and nodded but made no effort to get out of her car.

"Would you like to come in?" Desiree asked her, though she already knew the answer. It was clear that Zinga disliked Sandi on sight.

"No, love, I have to get home. There are a couple of things I need to take care of. I'll call you later."

Burning rubber, she zoomed off.

It was way past time for that talk with Sandi. Considering what she now knew, she could no longer put it off.

Desiree stood in the living room barring Sandi's progress as she tried to sidle by into the bedroom she'd pretty much taken over.

"Sandi, we really haven't had time to catch up. Let's have a glass of wine," Desiree suggested, trying to be pleasant.

Sandi tried stepping around her. "No wine for me. I'm here to take a quick shower and then I'm heading out."

Desiree placed a hand on her arm, stilling her. "This will only take a moment."

"I don't have a moment."

"You've been avoiding me," Desire accused, opting for the straight approach. "Maybe I should get right to the point. What are your plans?"

"Plans?" The actress raised a sculptured eyebrow.

"When are you leaving?"

Sandi now appeared visibly shocked. "Are you throwing me out? Is that what you're saying?"

Despite the fact her anger was slowly building, Desiree tried to keep her voice even. "You've been here going on two months and you don't seem too anxious to get back to work."

Sandi eyed her warily and took another step forward. Desiree met her halfway. She was practically in her face.

"What is this? I thought you enjoyed my company. I've been here to offer you support."

She really was nervy. Desiree decided to hold firm. "Hon, I'm starting to feel like you're using my home like a hotel and I'm beginning to feel used."

"How can you say that?" Sandi turned on the tears. She'd always been good at that. "I would never use you. We're old friends. Friends help each other out. I've paid rent. I figured you needed the money."

Sandi had paid her a pittance. She couldn't have gotten a room at No-tell Motel for a week for what she'd paid Desiree so far.

"Come on, sit down," Desiree urged, "just for a moment and we'll talk."

She moved over to the couch, hoping Sandi would follow. But Sandi's tears now turned into full-fledged sobs. She was actually sniveling and gasping.

"I have no place to go," she heaved out.

Desiree steeled herself not to back down; Sandi was an actress and a damn good one.

"How about going back to Amsterdam? I'm actively looking for a job. There's a good chance that once I get one, I'll be moving."

"Holland is not my home. Besides you don't have a job right now," Sandi cried. "Isn't this conversation premature?"

Desiree just wasn't getting through to her. Either that, or Sandi purposely didn't want to hear. She would stick to the point and not back down.

"I want my home back. You've taken advantage of me. You've helped yourself to my clothing. You've taken my car. You don't even pick up after yourself. It's getting old, Sandi and I'm getting angry."

Sandi's tears immediately dried up. There was an ugly expression on her face as she glared at Desiree.

"So what you're saying is that my support of you over the years doesn't count for anything. I've always been here for you. I stood by you when no one else would. I was the one who took care of you when you got pregnant. Who helped you get rid of that baby?"

It was as if she'd slapped Desiree's face.

"Rid of my baby?" Desiree shouted. "How can you even say that? You know the agony I went through."

Sandi's words had produced an ache in her gut, dredging up memories she would rather forget. What a bitch she was! How dare she say she helped her "get rid" of her child? Desiree's pregnancy had been unplanned, but that didn't mean she didn't want or love that baby. Had circumstances been different, she would have done almost anything to see that child grow up.

The baby had been the reason she'd agreed to make that horrible film. To think she'd gone through that demeaning experience for nothing; in the end she hadn't even gotten paid. The proceeds were supposed to be enough to allow her to keep her daughter. The jerk she'd gotten herself involved with hadn't stuck around when he found out she was pregnant. And she'd thought she was in love.

Desiree took a deep breath and tried to calm down. Sandi's insensitivity was unbelievable. After all these years, she was still trying to keep Desiree beholden to her. What did it matter now if Sandi blabbed the news that she'd sold her child? Desiree no longer worked for Fannie Jackson and her reputation was already shot. What did it matter?

"I want you out of my house tonight," Desiree said through gritted teeth. "I want you gone."

Sandi turned on the waterworks again. "You must be joking! I have no place to go."

"Sure you do. Try Byron, and if he doesn't bite, try that other guy, Glenn, or whatever his name is. If neither wants you, book yourself into a hotel. You've got money."

Desiree walked off, not caring that the mortgage was due. She didn't care if she'd have to use what was left of her savings to make it through until she found a job. She just wanted Sandi out.

A strangled gasp came from behind her. Unfortunately, she made the mistake of looking back.

"Please, Desiree," Sandi pleaded. "We've been friends for a long time. I was too embarrassed to tell you this. but I lost my job, too. I really have nowhere to go and I have no marketable skills."

And just like that, the truth had come out. Maybe. Desiree couldn't tell whether Sandi was lying or not.

CHAPTER 18

"Thanks for the tip. I'll definitely jump on it. Sounds like an excellent opportunity," Rafiq said.

Out of the blue, a teacher named Larry who'd taught with him a few years back in New Jersey had called to chat. As one thing led to another Rafiq told him about his situation. Larry then mentioned there were openings on the faculty of the small community college in Monmouth County where he taught.

While Rafiq preferred working with teenagers, he couldn't be too picky. A job was a job. Out of guilt and some misplaced sense of obligation, he still paid alimony to his ex-wife, who'd never remarried. That situation would continue for another two years. He was fairly confident his credentials and past experience teaching at a community college would give him an edge.

Besides, Red Bank was a charming shore town. In terms of locale he could do far worse than cute sidewalk cafés, interesting boutiques and sprawling Victorian homes. Plus, it was only an hour and a half from New York, which made it especially desirable.

Outside in the den, Desiree was definitely on a roll. He could hear the tip tap of her fingers as she typed. She was really into what she was doing. Every now and then she mumbled something out loud.

The more time he spent with her, the more Rafiq realized how attracted he was to Desiree. But he'd reined himself in. It was one thing to go for a walk and indulge in a little lovemaking, another to have her in his home, working. He didn't want to overstep his boundaries lest it be construed that he was taking advantage of the employer/employee thing.

While he wasn't a member of corporate America, or even a small business owner, it just didn't seem right for him to act on his feelings. And even though he was only paying a pittance, grocery money at best, technically he was still Desiree's employer. What she thought of him was important. He didn't want to be labeled a pig or a man with ulterior motives.

Drawn to the tip tapping of the keyboard, Rafiq headed toward the den. He entered the room silently and stood looking at Desiree hunched over the desk. Even in that position, there was a definite elegance to the way she sat. He admired the slope of her back through the thin cotton shirt and his eyes roamed the nape of her neck; a neck that he would rain soft kisses on if he had his way.

Desiree had pulled her hair high into a ponytail that swished back and forth as she typed. She must have sensed him standing behind her, because she turned and smiled.

"Was there something you wanted?" she asked.

The gleam in her mink-colored eyes drew Rafiq closer. She was becoming more relaxed every day. There was an indefinable sparkle and a hint of mischief in those eyes he found most appealing.

"I thought I'd check on you and see if you wanted a drink," he said.

She pointed to the bottle of water next to her. "No, thanks. I have plenty of water left."

Rafiq stood over her shoulder peering at the monitor as she continued to type. He was unable to concentrate as the alluring scent of a tantalizing perfume tickled his nostrils. Succumbing to the pull of the scent that reminded him of flowers, he rested his hands on her shoulders. Desiree shifted slightly and scooted her chair back, allowing him to see the computer screen.

"So what do you think?" she asked after a while when he remained silent.

"Looks like things are finally shaping up. I've got some newspaper articles about bipolar disorder in that box over there. You might want to go through them. The information should add more credibility to my book."

Desiree looked where he pointed. A file box was stacked against one wall, nearly overflowing. Over the years, Rafiq had collected articles from newspapers and periodicals. John's diagnosis had made him realize he knew very little about the disease. Now he read everything he could get his hands on.

"Come on, take a break," Rafiq said, his fingers stroking her nape. "What about coffee—will you have some?"

"I can make it if you'd like."

"Already done."

He hurried into the kitchen, retrieved the pot and two mugs and returned to her side.

"You've been busy," Desiree said. "I hardly see you anymore."

"I've been interviewing," Rafiq admitted. "Let's not forget I joined the ranks of the unemployed."

"Didn't Harvey offer you a job?"

Rafiq grunted. "Yes, he did, but I turned him down. It wasn't quite what I wanted."

"A job is a job. Right now I would take just about anything."

Rafiq rested his butt against the kitchen counter and crossed his arms. "I guess I still have a sour taste in my mouth because of the way this whole thing was handled. I wouldn't feel good working for an outfit that values connections over credentials."

"You're referring to Conrad's connection to Harvey's wife?"

Rafiq drained the last of the coffee from his cup. "You got it. Enough about me. What about you—any opportunities looming on the horizon?"

Desiree told him about the interview that had been so promising, but since then she hadn't heard a word.

"Something's got to break," Rafiq said, smiling down at her. "And what about that friend of yours?"

She shot him a look.

"The one who kept calling me. Is she still around?"

"I gave her two weeks to find a place to live. Much as I wanted to, I couldn't just throw her out on the street."

Rafiq pried himself away from the counter. He patted her shoulder awkwardly. "You're a soft touch. In this dog-eat-dog world, compassion is rare. I like it."

"My being a soft touch has gotten me nowhere," Desiree said half-jokingly.

"It's made you special, in my book."

She actually blushed and looked away.

Rafiq liked this soft side of Desiree. There was vulnerability hidden inside that tough outer shell. The thought occurred to him that she would make a wonderful mother.

He stood and picked up his empty cup. "I'll leave you to get back to business, then. I have errands to run."

Desiree scrunched up her nose, clearly puzzled. "Did I say something? Do something?"

He smiled. She should only know how deeply his feelings ran for her. He'd been envisioning her with child, his child—something he hadn't thought about for a while. Rafiq had convinced himself he'd never go there again. Bipolar disorder ran in families. It was genetically based. He'd heard it often enough from his ex, who'd blamed John's illness and subsequent suicide on him.

"If you're around when I get back we'll go to dinner," Rafiq offered.

"I'd like that." Desiree seemed both surprised and pleased by the invitation. "That box should keep me occupied most of the afternoon."

She rose, picked up her cup, and settled back into the chair in front of the computer.

"How's your dad?" Rafiq asked as he was turning away.

Desiree expelled a deep breath. "Nothing's really changed. I spoke to my mother earlier. There's discussion about moving him into a rehabilitation home." She squinted at Rafiq. "How did you know Terrence Mason was my father? I asked you that before and you ignored me."

"I have my ways."

"Don't give me that."

"Okay, okay. Years ago I specialized in Black Studies. I worshipped the ground both Martin Luther King Junior and Terrence Mason walked on. They had different philosophies but I admired them both and, naturally, I took interest in those fighting for the cause. Besides, I saw that photograph on your desk at school, the one of you as a little girl, standing with your parents and siblings. Recognizing Dr. Mason, I put two and two together."

"And came up with four," Desiree said, watching him, her eyes still narrowed. "I look nothing like that little girl in the picture."

"Your smile hasn't changed. Plus you look a lot like your father."

She seemed shocked.

Rafiq patted his back pocket and, reassured that he had his wallet, headed out. "We'll talk more over dinner," he said over his shoulder. "I'm curious to hear what it was like growing up in a family with political ties."

"It wasn't all peaches and cream," Desiree mumbled under her breath.

"*Life* isn't all peaches and cream." He raised a finger to his lips. "Save it for later."

Having said that, he quickly left.

Desiree waited until she was sure he'd left before she began tackling the paper-filled box. She decided to make herself comfortable, and sat cross-legged on the carpet sorting through newspapers and periodicals and putting them in chronological order.

Should she believe Rafiq? Had he really made the connection between the little girl in the photo and the adult she'd become? She supposed she wouldn't fully trust him until she found out who'd sent Harvey Coleman that tape.

Curiosity forced Desiree to do more than scan some of the articles. She was surprised to find that anxiety was listed as one of the symptoms of bipolar disorder. She learned that at times it was difficult to diagnose the symptoms in children. They usually did not fit the criteria established for adults.

Desiree continued to read.

At the bottom of the box there were several clippings bundled together. Removing the elastic band, she gave each a quick glance. They didn't seem to have relevance. Why would Rafiq save these fading accounts of some idiot who'd gotten himself arrested because he'd driven drunk? Then she read the headline on one of them and realized that the idiot was Rafiq.

Schoolteacher Arrested For DUI And Sentenced To Six Months Community Service.

The reporter did not paint a pretty picture of the man who had in so many ways been her savior. Rafiq had a past. It was not the first time he'd been pulled over for erratic driving. His license had been suspended before. Because there were extenuating circumstances—a recent death in the family—his lawyer had orchestrated a plea bargain and he'd been ordered by the court to attend Alcoholics Anonymous meetings. John's suicide was mentioned briefly.

Desiree felt like a voyeur reading the account, but somewhere deep down she needed to know. She ignored the tug in her gut and tried to envision what it must have been like to come home, open your garage door and find your teenage son swinging from a rafter. A sight like that would have had her in therapy for years.

Yet Rafiq seemed to have his act together. He'd somehow managed to move on, and he didn't drink. Desiree now understood this all-consuming need to document his experiences and share them with the world.

She returned the articles to exactly where she'd found them in the stash and secured them with the same elastic band, shoving them back into the box. She could pretend she'd never seen them, she supposed. She was in no position to judge. Everyone, she was beginning to find out, had a secret, and some might see hers as pretty sordid.

Rafiq was to be admired, she decided. She'd never once heard him bemoan his lot.

Desiree's focus returned to what was left in the box. She'd been working for almost an hour when her cell phone rang. Hitting the button without glancing at caller ID she picked up the call.

"Desiree?" The female voice sounded muffled. A plaintive sob ripped from the woman's throat. It took Desiree a second to realize it was Tanya. "Mother needs you. You need to come home."

Desiree pinched the bridge of her nose. She'd been expecting something like this and was surprised it hadn't come sooner.

"Did...uh...he have another stroke?" she asked.

"Actually, several little ones. His doctors say it's not good."

"Where's Mom now?"

"She won't leave his side. She's convinced her presence helps keep him alive."

"What about Terrence? Is he with you?"

Desiree feared the answer. Terrence had made it crystal clear he wanted little to do with the situation.

Tanya's sigh said it all. "He's come by a time or two, but he refuses to see Dad."

Desiree's conscience warred with her. She was torn between duty and a desire to run as far away as she could. But, as always, duty won out.

"I'll be there as soon as I can," she said, disconnecting and quickly shutting down the computer.

She scribbled a quick note to Rafiq, picked up her purse and hurried home to throw a few things into a bag.

At the house she made a number of calls. The first to Delta Airlines securing a flight, and the next to Zinga, who was not home. Desiree left her a message telling her what was going on. Sandi, as usual, was nowhere to be found, so Desiree scribbled another note.

She quickly depressed the button on the answering machine and listened to her messages. Maybe someone had called her for an interview.

Desiree waded through the canned voices of solicitors and then, finally, bingo! The school in Chesapeake had called. A too-enthusiastic secretary asked her to return the call to set up another interview. She should be elated, but her thoughts were now consumed with finding the quickest route to the airport.

Even Conrad Maloney's voice didn't make her bat an eye. Conrad would have to wait until she got back.

An hour later, boarding pass in hand, Desiree waited in the airport lounge with a group of grumbling passengers. The inbound flight was late, leaving them with no plane.

Desiree phoned Terrence Junior to advise him of the situation. He'd agreed to pick her up, and this time she hadn't protested. She was actually looking forward to seeing him and having his support.

"How is...he?" Desiree asked the moment Terrence answered.

Terrence's voice grew somber. Desiree wondered what was going on in his head "The doctors don't think he'll last the night, sis. Mother's a mess and Tanya, well, Tanya's being Tanya. She's made a list of things to take care of and she's assigned us chores."

The laughter that followed was far from lighthearted.

It sounded as if she might soon be without a father. Not that Terrence Senior had ever been the kind of father she'd hoped for. Still, it was sobering to realize that Ella might be the only parental figure she had left. Estranged or not, she'd taken her family for granted and assumed that they would always be there. It was time to pull herself together.

"Has Father discussed how his arrangements should be handled?" Desiree asked curiously. The control freak in Terence Senior would have listed every detail. "Does he want to be cremated or does he want a traditional funeral?"

"I'm sure you know the answer. Do you really think he's the type to pass up pomp and splendor?" Terrence said sourly. "He'd expect the works. How are you holding up?"

"I'm fine, actually. I sensed it was coming."

"Call me right before you board," Terrence said. "I'll be there to get you no matter the time." Then he hung up.

Desiree, carrying her hand luggage with her, wandered off to find a cup of coffee. It would be one long night, and caffeine would help her cope.

Coffee in hand, she found a seat in the lounge, and then, of course, her cell phone began to ring. She glanced at the caller ID and the name she saw there made her smile. Rafiq might very well be the only bright spot in what was turning out to be a dismal day.

"You got my note?" she inquired the moment she picked up. "I'm sorry I had to cancel our dinner plans."

"I did. And no, Desiree, I am the one who's sorry. I know it's tough."

"Rain check for dinner, then?" she asked, her voice growing soft.

"Rain check it is. Your priority right now is to support

your family. I'm not going anywhere. I'll be waiting here when you get back."

Desiree smiled, thinking Rafiq Jones was turning out to be a prince of a man.

CHAPTER 19

At last Desiree's flight was finally called. She boarded with a grumpy group of passengers and, after a bumpy flight, touched down at Hartsfield-Jackson Atlanta International Airport.

She'd packed only the essentials, just enough to see her through, God forbid if there was a funeral. She didn't plan on staying in Atlanta one day longer than necessary. She would help her mother and siblings with the funeral arrangements then hightail it out of there.

After exiting the secure area, Desiree spotted Terrence leaning against a post. Spotting her, he approached, and folded her into a stiff embrace.

"Good to see you again. Luggage?" he greeted.

Desiree shook her head.

"Shall we get going, then?"

"Any update?" Desiree asked, following him through the airport. Terrence's stolid features gave nothing away.

Her brother had always had a hangdog look about him that was hard to read. "It's not looking good," he tossed over his shoulder. Desiree was barely keeping up with his long strides. "The doctors say it's just a matter of time. The next stroke should put him out. He isn't even conscious."

"Then we need to hurry." Desiree caught up with Terrence and looped an arm through his elbow. She already dreaded what she would find when she got to the hospital, but she steeled herself to be strong.

Terrence Senior had been in pretty bad shape the last time she'd seen him. Desiree couldn't imagine how his appearance or condition could have gotten worse. While there were few fond memories of her father to look back on, she felt sorry for him. The way she now saw it, his passing might be a blessing in disguise. A man like her father would never be happy confined to a wheelchair or bed. He would hate relinquishing control.

Despite the slick roads, Terrence Junior drove like a madman. At last they pulled up in front of the hospital.

"Aren't you coming in?" Desiree asked. Terrence had made no effort to move. She felt as if this was déjà vu all over again. How could Terrence even think of just dropping her off?

He closed his eyes for a moment and seemed to debate. "Truthfully, I don't want to come in, though I suppose I should."

"You should. Park the car and I'll wait here," Desiree told him firmly. If she could put her personal feelings aside and travel to be with the family that had ostracized her, then, dammit, Terrence needed to step up to the plate. "Mother needs you," she said more gently, "and I could use your support."

Terrence muttered something and sighed, "I guess I'm the man in the family now. I'll do what I have to."

"You are. I'm getting out. I'll be waiting in the lobby."

Desiree got out of the BMW and slammed the door.

Terrence was back in less than ten minutes, a determined look on his face.

"Okay, let's do it," he said, taking her by the arm and walking with her into the elevator.

They got off on the eighth floor and almost ran into a visibly agitated Tanya pacing. She had a balled-up handkerchief in one hand and was dabbing at her eyes and crying

"It took you long enough to get here," she snapped. "You probably stopped off someplace to eat."

"We did not," Desiree said. "My flight was late. We got here as soon as we could. Where is Mother?"

Tanya's soft sobs punctuated her answer. "Mother had a panic attack. The doctor sedated her."

"And...our father? How is he?"

A choking sound escaped Tanya.

Desiree pretty much knew the answer.

"He passed away about half an hour ago."

"Why didn't you call me?" Terrence demanded, speaking up for the first time. "You have my cell phone."

"I thought it best to let you know in person." Tanya now began bawling in earnest and heads poked out from the surrounding rooms.

Terrence took long strides toward the nurses' station. "I need to talk to someone," he said, drumming his fingers against the Formica barrier and getting the attention of the same large nurse Desiree had run into before, the one who'd quizzed her with some skepticism.

"I'll page the attending doctor for you," she said, taking a step back from him and hugging a clipboard to her ample bosom. "If you'll wait in the lounge, Dr. Hoffman will speak with you."

"How long will this take?" Terrence demanded. "I'd like to see my mother."

Tanya, meanwhile, had dissolved in sobs and Desiree placed a comforting arm around her sister's shoulders.

"I know. I know," she crooned. "You should call Ron and have him take you home."

But Tanya could not or would not stop crying. It was as if the floodgates had opened up and months, maybe years, of anguish were pouring out.

"I'm finding a vending machine and getting us coffee," Terrence said, as if that would make the situation better. Desiree suspected he needed the time to pull himself together.

"The lounge has coffee," the poker-faced nurse pointed out. "Why don't I take you there?" She began corralling them. Desiree suspected she wanted them away from the other patients and guests.

The next few hours passed in a blur. Desiree vaguely remembered a young female doctor speaking with them and telling them that their father had had a massive stroke. She remembered Tanya's high-pitched keening and Terrence's quiet acceptance of things. He'd called Tanya's husband, urging him to come and take his wife home. Then, with an amazing calmness, he'd taken over.

Ella had gone through the motions required of her. She'd numbly described her husband's last living moments. After a while, they'd all been persuaded to go home to begin the daunting task of making funeral arrangements.

The funeral occurred three days later, complete with police escorts and most of Atlanta. The service, an orchestrated event, went on forever and ever. The minister, a family friend, droned on and on, singing Terrence Senior's praises and reminding everyone how instrumental he'd been to the black movement.

"My daddy's gone," Tanya frequently sobbed, collapsing on the hard wooden pew while the choir, decked out in purple and white robes, belted hymns so poignant the congregation frequently dissolved into tears.

Through it all, a heavily sedated Ella performed like a trouper, accepting heartfelt condolences while fighting back tears.

Terrence Junior had moved into the family home temporarily. He'd been the one to ensure the father he hated had the proper send-off. He remained at the graveside, the perfect son, supporting his mother and Tanya as the coffin was lowered into the ground.

Desiree somehow managed to remain dry-eyed throughout it all. Too numb to even cry, she didn't pretend to mourn a man who had in no shape or form ever been a father to her. She stoically accepted the condolences of friends and relatives she vaguely remembered. Then, later, she returned to the house to help serve up the enormous feast Winnetta had prepared, listening with one ear as grieving acquaintances recounted endless tales of Terrence Senior's benevolence.

And, finally, it was all over. She was free to return to Bethesda to pick up her life. Terrence Junior had agreed to stay on with Ella for as long as she needed him.

Satisfied that her mother would be taken care of, Desiree boarded the plane taking her back to Bethesda.

When she got home, she entered her condo to find bags and boxes stacked at the door. Hallelujah, Sandi was leaving. And not a minute too soon.

"Sandi," Desiree called. "Where are you?"

No answer.

"Sandi!"

Setting her bags down, Desiree set off to find the woman she'd once considered a friend. A brief look around the place yielded no signs of another occupant and, true to form, Sandi's room was a mess. She'd packed up hastily, leaving behind paper bags, shoe boxes and a carpet flecked with lint.

No point in getting irritated now. At least she was meeting her two-week deadline and there would not be another unpleasant confrontation. It was the best welcome-home gift Desiree could get. Although it was mid-afternoon she headed for bed.

Several hours must have elapsed when Desiree, who'd fallen asleep, heard noises outside. Woozy, she crawled from under the covers and went off to investigate.

"You scared me," Sandi accused, immaculately attired as always. The actress placed a hand on her chest. "When did you get back?"

"A few hours ago. What's this?" Desiree asked, pointing at the stacked bags.

"I'm leaving," Sandi reminded her. "You were pretty firm on that point. You wanted me gone."

"Where to?"

Sandi shrugged. "I'm staying with a friend."

A man's voice came from the vicinity of the open door. "Babe, are you ready?"

A tall man, someone Desiree vaguely recognized, entered. "Glenn Browne," he said, sticking out his hand.

The man at the airport. The one Sandi had been chatting up.

"I'm sorry about your father," he said, a smile creasing his face. "Sandi has told me quite a bit about you."

Desiree accepted his condolences and watched as he began gathering Sandi's things. She wondered what else Sandi had told him. It didn't much matter now, anyway.

"Call me if I've left anything behind," Sandi said breezily. "You've got my cell number. By the way, some guy called Conrad keeps phoning. He left a message. We finally connected last night and I told him you were out of town."

She swept through the apartment, looking to see if she'd left anything behind. Convinced there was nothing visible, Sandi picked up one tiny bag and said to Glenn, who was starting to look like a pack mule, "Well, that's that. We're off."

Desiree accepted Sandi's perfunctory hug and air kiss.

"We'll do lunch sometime," the actress promised.

Desiree simply nodded and smiled. She doubted that would happen. Sandi, who still owed rent money, made no mention of it.

Finally she was gone and Desiree was left to clean up the havoc she'd wreaked.

Wide-awake now, she decided to return Conrad Maloney's call. He'd been persistent, and she couldn't imagine what he wanted with her, since she no longer served a useful purpose. She had no helpful contacts he could use.

After quickly punching in the digits, she waited. Conrad picked up almost instantaneously.

"So how have you been?" he asked, having clearly checked his own caller ID.

"Life could be better. What's new with you?"

"I thought you might have heard about my appointment."

Desiree waited for him to go on, but he did not elaborate.

"I take it you're speaking of the dean's position?" she said, taking the bull by the horns.

"Yes. I've been meaning to call you, but life got in the way."

"When did you decide to apply for Harvey's job?" Desiree asked. "And why didn't you tell me?"

The silence on the other end spoke volumes. At last Conrad said, "I didn't think I had a shot, even though I was asked to apply."

"Who asked you?" Desiree challenged. Conrad's responses so far sounded like a bunch of BS to her.

"Does it matter?"

"Matters to me. I applied for that position. You knew it. You even helped me plan my strategy."

"I don't recall," Conrad answered.

Desiree was tired of going around in circles. She was emotionally exhausted from her long day and in no mood for games.

"Conrad," she said, getting directly to the point, "you and I had a standard lunch date. We talked and talked, yet you never once mentioned that we were both up for the same position. I have to wonder why."

"I never saw myself as a serious contender," Conrad explained again. "Everyone at Fannie Jackson thought you walked on water. I figured you had it all sewn up, so there wasn't any need to bring it up."

What gall, and how underhanded!

"And to make sure I didn't have it sewn up, you tried to discredit me," Desiree said, putting it right out there.

"What are you talking about?"

"I'm talking about your attempt to sabotage me." Desiree said, cutting him no slack. "You did some digging, found an old video and sent it to Harvey."

"I did not."

Conrad was actually starting to lose his cool. A first. She'd pushed a hot button. She'd continue pushing.

"So what is it you want now, Conrad? You want to gloat?"

He sighed loudly. "My, aren't you the suspicious one. I hoped to reconnect with my old friend. I heard you were looking for a job and I thought I might be able to help."

Desiree wondered if Conrad was feeling guilty. Now that he had the job, she was no longer in his way and he could afford to be magnanimous. She remained quiet, letting him ramble on. While she might be desperate to find work, she'd be damned if she'd be beholden to him in any way.

Desiree waited until he wound down before playing her ace card, "So Conrad, is it true you're related to Harvey's wife?"

His audible intake of breath made her realize she'd hit a nerve, then Conrad rallied. "Just what are you implying?"

"Nothing. Merely asking."

"Clearly I've wasted my time trying to help you," he said coldly. "I wish you the best."

The phone disconnected, leaving Desiree with the dial tone reverberating in her ear.

He'd wanted something from her. Desiree meant to find out just what.

CHAPTER 20

"I've accepted a job in New Jersey," Rafiq announced, setting his glass of Lassie down. "The pay is surprisingly good and this will be like going home."

"I'm happy for you," Desiree said, knowing deep down that she'd miss him. She sipped the yogurt-based drink he'd introduced her to and asked, "When do you start?"

"In August, which gives us most of the summer to work on my book. Anything happening with you?"

Desiree shook her head. She was delighted for Rafiq, yet envious at the same time. In a few days she would have a second interview with the private school in Chesapeake, but that didn't mean she had a job, and her funds were rapidly dwindling.

Taking a moment to collect her thoughts, she gazed around the outdoor garden of the charming Indian restaurant Rafiq had chosen. He'd said he wanted something different and special for their dinner date.

"Things are pretty much status quo on my end," Desiree finally answered. "I've sent résumés out, but so far I've only had one nibble. The school did call me back for a second interview, so we'll see."

"That's the school in Chesapeake?"

She nodded. "Yes. I suppose I could do worse. It's a lovely area and the people I met on the faculty are nice."

"Monmouth County in New Jersey is also beautiful. My buddy Larry mentioned there were still openings on the faculty. Maybe you should consider applying."

"Maybe I will," Desiree said, digging into her spicy lamb vindaloo. She had nothing to lose and, since Rafiq had already been hired, she would be working with someone she knew. "This is delicious and definitely hot."

"I thought you might like it."

The restaurant offered beer and wine, but Rafiq had passed, ordering Lassie for them both. Having no desire to drink alone, Desiree had accepted his choice.

She'd never mentioned that she knew he'd been arrested for DUI. That was a delicate subject and, in some ways, she'd felt that by reading that article she'd invaded his privacy. But curiosity got the better of her now. She needed to know what had happened.

"Rafiq, I've never seen you drink. How come?"

He set down his knife and fork and looked her in the eye. "Is that a problem?" A disarming smile followed.

"Not a problem at all. I'm just curious."

"I don't drink because at one time my drinking was way out of control."

"Did you start drinking before or after your son died?" she probed.

"Way before." Rafiq's attention turned to his plate. He picked up his fork and began attacking his tandoori chicken as if it were still living and might easily fly away.

The fork fell again with a clatter.

"You want the truth? I began drinking heavily when it was evident my marriage was over. The drinking worsened after John died. I drank to ease pain and it helped me cope during a difficult time."

"Oh, Rafiq, it must have been rough. Who could blame you?" Desiree said, her compassion kicking in. She reached across the table and took his hand. "I would probably have done the same thing if I'd been in your position."

And she had been in a similar position. She'd lost a child but not to death. Instead of drinking, she'd busied herself with education classes hoping that eventually she would earn a decent living. If she ever got pregnant again she would have the means to raise a child alone.

"There's no excuse for almost killing a man," Rafiq muttered under his breath.

"I don't understand. When did that happen?"

"Back in New Jersey. I drove under the influence. I

should never have been behind the wheel of a car. The silver lining is that I was forced to attend Alcoholics Anonymous meetings. I credit that organization for putting me back on track."

Desiree's conscience warred with her. Should she tell him that she'd read about his arrest while she was sorting through that box, or should she keep her mouth shut? After mentally debating, she elected to leave well enough alone.

"Are you still attending meetings?" Desiree asked when the silence stretched out.

Rafiq took another sip of Lassie. "Yes, whenever I can. Getting arrested was a wake-up call. Shall we talk about something less depressing? What's happening with your friend these days? Have you heard from her since she moved out?"

"Not a word. But that's not a surprise."

The conversation shifted to Desiree's efforts to find a job. Rafiq kept urging her to apply to the school in New Jersey. She noticed that the rest of his meal remained untouched.

When they were on their second cup of coffee, Rafiq appeared to return to his old self. "Did you ever find out who sent Harvey that video?" he asked.

Desiree went instantly on the alert. Was she about to hear a confession?

"No, I still don't know. I confronted Conrad Maloney, but he vehemently denied it."

Rafiq raised an eyebrow. "That's hardly a surprise. What else would he do?"

"You're right, I suppose. It wouldn't matter anyway. My reputation has already been ruined."

The waitress hovered.

"Would you like anything else?" Rafiq asked Desiree politely.

When she shook her head, he signaled for the check. That business out of the way, he stood and offered her his arm. "How about we walk off those calories? The gardens look particularly inviting now that the sun is going down."

Others had a similar idea. Adults strolled the paths admiring the flowers while their children skipped ahead.

Desiree kept her hand tucked in the crook of Rafiq's arm as they continued to stroll. When they came to a gazebo, he stopped. He subtly shifted positions until Desiree was facing him.

"What if I told you I find you attractive?"

It was such an abrupt shift in conversation, Desiree couldn't think of a thing to say.

"Am I embarrassing you?"

"Uh, no. I'm flattered and totally speechless."

He cupped her chin forcing her to look at him. "Do you think there might be hope for us?"

Rafiq's declaration coming as it did out of left field, was a lot to digest. Desiree had thought he'd lost interest. There'd been no repeat of that romantic evening which now seemed eons ago.

He was waiting for her to say something an expectant look on his face.

"We're spending more and more time together," Desiree said finally. "What you've shown me so far I definitely like."

"So you're saying you're interested?"

"I am. But I'm not sure why you'd be interested in me? You could do a lot better."

She knew he could. A man of a certain age never lacked for female companionship.

"Why do you say that?" Rafiq asked, pressing her palm to his lips.

She sighed. "Because I've made a mess of my life and I'm unemployed."

"You've had a momentary setback. You're bright, beautiful and accomplished. And I'm not exactly a prize. I have a failed marriage behind me and I failed my son. I've lost everything I've worked for. You're speaking to a man with no tangible assets except for a few pennies saved."

Desiree took a deep breath. "That night when you kissed me, I knew I cared."

He seemed pleased by her declaration. "You're coming out of a long-term relationship. Sure you're not on the rebound?" he asked.

Desiree hadn't thought about her relationship with Byron in some time. She'd been comfortable with him, but not necessarily in love.

"It's been over for a while," she admitted. "In retrospect, Byron did me a huge favor."

Rafiq seemed relieved. He tugged her inside the gazebo and cut off what she was about to say with what could only be described as a heart-stopping kiss. A kiss Desiree was reluctant to end.

When she finally came up for breath, Desiree had decided he was worth a shot. A relationship with this man, long-distance or otherwise, was definitely worth exploring.

That annoying friend of Desiree's was the first person Sandi spotted when the chauffeur helped her out of the limousine. She held her head high and decided to ignore her.

Glenn, his palm on the small of Sandi's back, guided her toward the entrance of the W Hotel.

They were attending a gala event put on by the NAACP to raise funds for college-bound youth. The crème de la crème of Maryland society had been invited and Sandi had pulled out all the stops. She was glamour personified, knowing that the press would be out in full force.

At five hundred dollars a head, the event had attracted a lot of attention; that was how it should be. These charities normally brought affluent movers and shakers. Sandi figured Glenn would never risk being seen with her if there was a wife in the picture.

The obnoxious woman, spotting them, peeled herself away from a chatting group of people. Her smile shifted a little as she gave Sandi the once-over. It was almost a sneer.

"May I have your invitation?" she said to Glenn, pointedly ignoring Sandi.

Glenn handed over the gold-embossed card which Zinga carefully scrutinized.

"Please follow me," she said, her lips curled.

They were led to a table up front already occupied by six people. When Zinga moved off to greet another couple, Sandi thought she heard her mumble under her breath, "I was expecting a better class of people."

Sour grapes, Sandi decided. The woman was bellyaching because she was jealous and only the hired help.

Easing into the seat Glenn held out, Sandi nodded as introductions were made.

"You'll never guess who's here," Zinga said excitedly. She pointed a finger to a table up front.

Desiree's attention was still on the entrance. "Since when have you ever been starstruck?"

"I'm not swooning over some so-called celebrity. I'm still in shock. Didn't you see Sandi? She's draped all over some guy who's finer than Denzel."

Desiree finally took notice.

"Sandi is here?"

"Yes, ma'am, seated at table four. That woman sure knows how to work it."

It was all Desiree needed. Zinga had persuaded her to

volunteer as a hostess. She'd agreed because there wasn't a more worthwhile cause she could think of. Sitting at home waiting for the phone to ring was getting old. Two weeks had gone by, the second interview was behind her, and she still hadn't heard a word.

Zinga now elbowed her. "Look who else is here. You want him?"

Desiree squinted in the direction Zinga was staring. She spotted a portly dark-skinned man in a too-tight tuxedo with what was clearly a trophy on his arm.

"Am I supposed to know him?"

"Not tubby and the string bean," Zinga hissed. "Byron over there with that white woman."

Desiree zeroed in on Byron at the same time he spotted her. He seemed to visibly pale but rallied and flashed his professional smile.

"He's mine," Desiree said, making a beeline toward her ex.

"Byron," Desiree greeted. "May I see your invitation?"

He seemed to debate, then reluctantly turned over the card. His glance flickered over the formal black pantsuit she wore.

"You're looking good, Desiree. Why do you need my invitation?"

Desiree held out her hand, her smile equally bright. "I'm working the event. I'm your hostess."

The blonde accompanying Byron regarded her curiously. Who knew whether she was a business date or otherwise?

"Table three is in a good location," Desiree offered, leading the way. "You'll have a terrific view of the dais and speakers."

Byron took the blonde's hand and followed Desiree. She deliberately led them by table four, where Sandi was seated. Desiree was forced to admit her ex-roommate's strapless blue gown was an attention getter. Oblivious to their proximity, she conducted an animated conversation with the man to her left.

Desiree tapped Sandi's bare shoulder. Sandi turned and flashed her movie-star smile. When she spotted Desiree with Byron and his date in tow, that smile turned into a frown.

"What a surprise to see you, Sandi," Desiree said, and quickly moved on.

Byron's expression was thunderous.

"Have fun," Desiree said as he and the blonde took their seats.

People were now coming in dribs and drabs. Desiree, still stunned at having to deal with both Byron and Sandi, returned to her post to greet the remaining arrivals. Oh, to be a fly on the wall and witness the drama. Byron and Sandi were clearly on the outs. Neither seemed particularly pleased to see the other.

A gray limousine pulled up and an attractive middle-aged woman stepped out, followed by two men.

"Desiree," the woman called, waving at her. "Just look at you. You look wonderful." She openly admired Desiree's pantsuit with the sequined collar and matching bustier before turning to one of the men flanking her. "Look who's here, Harvey."

Harvey Coleman quickly recovered. He placed an arm around his wife's shoulders and smiled at Desiree. Conrad Maloney, the other man, didn't even look over.

"How are you doing?" Harvey said somewhat brusquely.

Perfunctory as his greeting was, Desiree saw no point in not being gracious.

"Quite well, Harvey. Do you know where your table is?"

He removed an invitation from the inside pocket of an immaculate black tuxedo and handed it over.

Desiree glanced at the elegant card. She slanted an eye in Conrad's direction, but he stared straight ahead.

"Please follow me," she said.

Steps from their table, Harvey placed a hand on her arm.

"It's going to be tough replacing you. I'm sorry our association ended the way it did. By the way, that school in Chesapeake called. I gave you a glowing recommendation, and I destroyed that incriminating tape."

"Thank you," Desiree said, meaning it. Hopefully, Harvey's word would count for something.

She hurried off, thinking Harvey had actually been decent. Wished she could say the same for Conrad.

Yet this particular encounter had left her shaken. It seemed her entire life had converged in one room, but at least she was beginning to achieve closure.

Desiree had come to realize how pathetic Sandi really was. The actress needed a man to validate her existence and she was not above using people to get her way. She'd relinquished her power to this woman, allowing her to call the shots.

Desiree would always regret giving up her baby, but it wasn't a crime to put a child up for adoption. It wasn't as if she'd sold her to the highest bidder. She could hold her head high. Sure, she'd accepted the money the adoptive parents had offered to pay her medical expenses, but there was no shame to what she had done.

Byron's presence, and her reaction to him, also made her realize it was finally over. And seeing Harvey and Conrad was a reminder she was still unemployed. Time to take back control of her life and act on Rafiq's suggestion. She would send off her résumé to that college in New Jersey.

She returned to the business of meeting and greeting. Once the event was well underway, and everyone seated, she and Zinga were finally able to talk.

"Did I tell you a new English teacher's been hired?" her friend said.

Desiree shook her head and quipped, "Must have slipped your mind."

"Your replacement comes from Conrad's old school."

"What a surprise."

"Aren't you mad? Conrad was probably attempting to reach you so he could find out where you kept your lesson plans. Your replacement had to be his choice."

Desiree shrugged. It no longer mattered. She should be angry, she supposed, but the truth was that nothing Conrad did mattered anymore.

"Uh, oh," Zinga chortled, changing the subject. "Fireworks are on."

Desiree followed the direction of her friend's gaze. Sandi had made her way over to Byron's table and the two were conducting what looked to be a heated conversation.

"I'm going to go over," Zinga said, giving Desiree her Cheshire cat grin.

"Why bother?" Desiree was sick to death of the drama and wished that Zinga would leave well enough alone.

Her friend held up a sparkly rhinestone bracelet. "Look, someone lost this bauble in the ladies' room. I'll pretend I'm looking for the owner."

"You're a mess."

"No, just nosey. If two people ever deserved each other, it's them."

Desiree couldn't agree more. Byron and Sandi were a match made in Beelzebub heaven.

Time to forget about these people and take some necessary steps.

She would definitely apply for that job in New Jersey.

CHAPTER 21

"Mother," Terrence yelled. "Can you come here for a moment?"

Terrence tried opening the file cabinet again, but not one drawer budged.

He'd spent most of the morning in his father's study, boxing up items that were to go to several charities. Ella, after giving it some thought, had agreed to sell the house.

Ella reluctantly stood at the door of the room that had once been her husband's haven. She placed a hand to her chest.

"I'm here, child. What is it you want?" she asked.

It still amazed him that, though he was forty-six years old, Ella so often referred to him as a child. But he supposed every parent thought of their offspring as children.

In the few weeks he'd moved back home they'd managed to establish an amazing rapport; he was even beginning to respect her. Ella was stronger than she let on. Now that her husband was gone she was slowly coming into her own

"Mom," Terrence said, "I'm almost through in here except for that one file cabinet. Do you have the keys?"

"Can't say that I do. Your father stashed his important papers in there. Tanya may have a set of keys. She's the one person he trusted. She was his favorite." The latter was said without bitterness.

Terrence was surprised Ella had so freely admitted it. While there was no love lost between him and his father, he wasn't sure how he felt about it.

"If you don't mind I'd rather not deal with Tanya." Tanya had made it clear that his moving back home, albeit temporary, was suspect. Terrence figured she viewed his presence as a threat to her inheritance. "What I'll do is pick the lock," he said.

"Do what you have to do," Ella answered, sounding distracted. "I'm helping Winnetta with dinner. She's got some new recipe she wants to try." With that she rushed off.

And who could blame her? The wood-paneled room probably held memories that were both painful and poignant. His father had spent a lifetime holed up in that room supposedly attending to business.

Fifteen minutes later, Terrence had successfully broken the lock. He stood for a moment looking at papers that had been meticulously arranged in date order. Sheer curiosity drove him to pick up one of the folders and peruse it.

He scanned the contents and quickly wheeled the cabinet over to an easy chair. Removing several files, he began perusing reports written by a private investigator. Each of the files chronicled some detail of Desiree's life.

The old man was amazing. He'd wanted to stay connected with his youngest daughter and had gone to enormous expense to do so. As Terrence continued to read he felt as if he was invading his youngest sister's life, the details of which he could have been spared. What did those videos in the back of the cabinet hold?

"Mother," Terrence called again, climbing out of the comfortable chair. "I need you."

"I'll be there in a few," Ella shouted back.

She showed up shortly after, wiping her hands on a kitchen towel. "What's wrong?"

Terrence noticed she made no attempt to enter the room. He crossed over and handed her a sheaf of papers. "Maybe you should read these yourself. If there's a video player around I'd like to see what these tapes are about."

Ella reluctantly entered the room and took the seat he'd vacated. Her face crumbled as she began reading the documents.

"Where did you find these...uh...papers?" she asked, sounding out of breath.

"In the locked file cabinet."

This time Ella began wheezing in earnest. Terrence growing concerned for her well-being offered, "I'll get you a glass of water. Meanwhile, take long, slow breaths."

"No. No. I'll be okay."

Although she protested, he wasn't so sure about that. Ella was perspiring and her entire body shook. Her lips had even turned purple. Keeping an eye on her, Terrence picked up two videocassettes and began looking around the room for a player.

"Over there," Ella pointed out. "On the bookshelves."

Terrence crossed over to the built-in bookcases. Sure enough, in the middle there was a television and video player. He inserted a tape.

A few minutes later, having seen enough, he snapped the player off.

Ella was clearly in shock. She nearly had the dry heaves.

"My Desiree?" she cried. "I don't think I've ever seen anything this vile." Tears were pouring down her face. "That child had to have been desperate for money. How could she have gotten herself into such a mess?"

And although Terrence had been rendered speechless by what he saw, he felt it was his duty to defend Desiree.

"You called it right, Mother. Desiree must have been desperate. And it was a long time ago, Mother. Picture a frightened runaway with no way to support herself. Father had to have gone through quite a bit of trouble, not to mention the expense, to get these from the PI he hired."

"He loved that child."

"Did he? But he never mentioned a word to you."

"He probably wanted to spare me."

Even in death Ella was still picking up for her husband. "I wonder if Tanya knew about this?" she muttered. Ella's hands clasped her head. "My poor, sweet, misguided Desiree."

Still holding the telltale cassette in one hand, Terrence picked up the telephone.

Ella now shot to her feet. "What are you doing?"

"Calling Tanya, Mother."

She sat down wearily again. "Tanya's not going to like this one bit."

"To hell with what she thinks."

Terrence was already punching in numbers. He clenched and unclenched his teeth waiting while the phone rang.

"Tanya?" Terrence said, the moment she answered. "How are you?"

"What do you want?" Her hostility came over loud and clear.

"What about 'How are you Terrence?'" he said, keeping his voice even. "Am I catching you at a bad time?"

"Cut the shit and get to the point," she snapped. "What is it you want?"

"No point in getting nasty. Let's at least attempt to be civil."

There was a whooshing sound on the other end as

Tanya blew out a breath. "Why? My attempts at civility ended when you moved into the house you couldn't wait to move out of. I'm onto you."

He refused to be baited into saying anything he'd later regret. His sister was one angry woman. Tanya had always been resentful of him and Desiree. Terrence suspected it had something to do with them escaping the household while she felt trapped. She'd gotten married at an early age, trading one controlling environment for another. Even so she'd played the dutiful martyr, attending every Sunday dinner, and remaining at her parents' beck and call.

"I'm packing up dad's office," Terrence said, cutting to the chase.

"What's that have to do with me?"

Terrence again bit his tongue. Tanya required patience. Patience he didn't have.

"I need the key to the file cabinet."

He heard another sharp intake of breath. It came over loud and clear. "What does that have to do with me?"

"Mother mentioned you might have it."

"Mother is wrong."

Terrence sensed Ella listening. She must be busy following the one-sided conversation. He turned and placed a finger to his lips.

"Then I'll have to break the lock."

"You wouldn't want to do that."

"Why not?"

Tanya had fallen right into his trap. He'd purposely placed the call to gauge her reaction and from her hostility, it was evident he'd gotten his answer. Tanya knew exactly what was in that file cabinet.

"Sorry I bothered you," he said hanging up.

The sounds of Ella's sobbing caused him to pause. He'd been considering calling Desiree.

"I hate it that my children are fighting," Ella said.

And although Terrence had never been one for much physical contact, he crossed over and held his mother in his arms.

The phone rang just as Desiree was getting ready for bed. Who could be calling at this time? Without checking caller ID, she reached for the phone.

"Desiree, sorry to call you at this late hour."

Terrence's voice rushed at her. Desiree tensed up, preparing herself for bad news. Her brother had stayed in touch, calling periodically to catch up, but he'd never phoned at this hour before.

"What's up?" she asked, stepping into the boxers she slept in.

"I'm flying into the D.C. area on business. I'm wondering if I can take you out to lunch."

"When are you coming?"

"Day after tomorrow. I figured school was out and you might be free. There's something I want to talk to you about."

Desiree still hadn't told the family she'd been fired.

"It would be nice to see you," she said. "How's Mom holding up?"

They talked a little bit about Ella before hanging up.

For the next couple of days Desiree busied herself sending out résumés. Acting on Rafiq's tip, she even sent one off to Monmouth College.

Meanwhile, they were making major headway on Rafiq's project. He'd already sent out letters to editors and agents and now waited to hear something back. Their daily routine had grown comfortable; while Rafiq typed, Desiree proofread the work he'd completed. And at the end of the day, as the sun was going down, the two of them ran.

They'd just returned from a lengthy jog and were in his kitchen sipping water when he surprised her by saying, "We never discussed children, Desiree. How do you feel? Are children something you want?"

Surprised at the sudden change of topic, she came close to choking on her water. Desiree set down the bottle and took a deep breath. It was now or never. Rafiq had no inkling she'd had a child and had given that child up for adoption.

Now how to phrase it? What would he think of her?

"I love children," Desiree said. "Why else would I have chosen teaching as a profession?"

"Some do it for the time off," Rafiq answered, his fingers stroking her forearm. "You, on the other hand, have this amazing ability to reach teenagers. You couldn't possibly have accomplished what you have if you didn't like kids. I've been doing a lot of thinking and I'd like to have another child someday. I just want to be sure we're both on the same wavelength."

"Are you proposing to me?" Desiree joked. "It's sort of putting the cart before the horse, since we haven't slept together yet."

"That can be easily remedied. Trust me, it's all I think about." He winked at her, then his expression grew serious. "There aren't that many weeks left before I leave for New Jersey. We need to make plans."

"What are you thinking?"

Desiree had figured their developing relationship might very well dissolve when Rafiq moved on. She'd hoped that wouldn't be so. But just in case, she'd been preparing herself.

"I'm proposing," Rafiq answered, "that even if you don't get a job at the college in New Jersey we continue on. If things go as I think they will, at some point one of us will have to make a decision."

All this talk about babies and decisions had Desiree's head spinning. Still, it was nice to know he was serious, that filled her with a warm glow. She was beginning to fall in love with Rafiq.

"I sent my résumé off to Monmouth College," Desiree admitted. "I'm not holding my breath, since I have no previous college teaching experience."

"But you do have a master's and excellent credentials," he pointed out. "That's got to count for something."

True. And if Harvey Coleman was willing to give her a good recommendation, then maybe anything was possible. Things suddenly didn't seem that bad after all.

Rafiq reached over to smooth back a lock of her hair. "Desiree," he said, "maybe we should consider taking this relationship to another level. I'd like nothing better than to make love to you."

She needed to tell him now about the child she had given up for adoption. It was a secret she'd hidden for far too long.

Desiree began tentatively, "You mentioned something about having children. What if I were to tell you I already had a child?"

He blinked at her. "Had? Where did that child disappear to?"

She'd gotten his attention now, all right. Rafiq's tawny eyes regarded her curiously. "You never mentioned you were married."

"I wasn't. I was seventeen years old and imagined myself in love. The man I was dating was old enough to be my father. I was naive enough to believe he cared about me."

Rafiq's palm stroked her cheek. It was an encouraging sign. So far he was handling this bombshell rather well. "Go on."

"The moment he heard I was pregnant he took off."

"Bastard! That must have been rough."

There was compassion in Rafiq's voice and, at the same time, barely concealed anger. Desiree had never articulated her feelings of hurt and abandonment to a single living soul. The way Rafiq looked at her gave her the courage to continue the sordid tale.

Choking back emotion, she said, "I had my baby and put her up for adoption. A couple from Cleveland who desperately wanted a child paid for my medical expenses and housing. In turn, I sold them my baby girl."

"You *gave* them your child, Desiree. You allowed that baby to have a better life than you could provide. It was a brave and sensible thing you did. You must still think about your daughter."

Despite her efforts to hold tears back, a few escaped. "Often, and, no, I didn't feel brave. I was desperate. That's how I got myself into this bind. There isn't a day that goes by that I don't wonder what my child looks like. And I question my decision. What if life hasn't been kind to her? What if I never have another baby?"

"You will." Rafiq said, hugging her to him. Desiree broke down and the tears spilled over. She couldn't believe how kind he was being. "What about this bind you're in?"

"It's the video that was sent to Fannie Jackson. I made a bad call because I needed money and wanted to keep my baby. Hooking up with Sandi at that audition seemed a blessing at that time. It was she who convinced me the film would be artsy and tasteful. Several well-known actresses had started out this way."

"Okay, so you made the movie and they paid you. How come you still gave up your baby?"

"Because I never got paid."

Rafiq snorted in disgust. "It was a scam. You went through all of that for nothing?"

"Afraid so. And the movie eventually got scrapped. I didn't even know a video existed until it surfaced."

"You poor child. I can't imagine having to go through all that by yourself."

Desiree's tears stopped. "Sandi was the only one there for me. I needed a place to live and she took me in."

"Ah, so that explains the relationship and why you felt you owed her. I wondered about that."

Rafiq pressed her head against his solid chest. The floodgates opened again and he didn't say a word, just let her sob.

After a few more minutes went by, Desiree dried her eyes on the tissue he handed her. "Look at me. I'm a mess," she said shakily.

"You're beautiful to me, and that cry was a long time coming. You needed to get that out." He pressed a kiss against her temple.

Desiree twined her hands around his neck. "Didn't you say something about wanting to take me to bed?"

"I did."

Stepping out of his embrace, she took him by the hand

and led him to the bedroom. She needed the comfort of his body and needed him to hold her. The first thing she noticed was the packed boxes, another sign he would be leaving her soon.

"Take your clothes off, baby," Rafiq said softly, beginning to step out of his. "Let me love you."

Desiree stripped off her clothes and crawled under the covers. Rafiq joined her and brought her close to his chest.

When he kissed her, all the old hurts seemed to disappear. He poured scented oil from a bottle into his palms and massaged her entire body until she finally relaxed. Then Desiree reciprocated, skillfully kneading his smooth flesh, focusing on where there were tension knots. He was all sinew and muscle. He smelled like Irish Spring soap and the beginnings of lovemaking.

Rafiq's mouth covered a nipple. His lips tugged and suckled, awakening in her a desire she hadn't felt in a long time. Her hands slid to his hip, her fingers moving in small circles. His loving continued until her center pulsated, and her breath came in erratic bursts. Gently he positioned her on her back and nudged her thighs apart.

He covered every inch of her body with wet kisses while his fingers probed the soft flesh between her legs. Sensations she'd never experienced came to the fore. She was drowning in him. Desiree had reached that point where the real world receded and only the two of them existed. He slid between her legs, his member teasing her opening. Unable to stop herself, Desiree whimpered and demanded to be satisfied.

His lips were on her stomach and his hands cupped her butt. She arched into him, needing to share the heat that now burned her up.

"Baby," Rafiq said, "I'll need to get a condom."

"Hurry up."

Desiree wanted him inside her, needed to feel as if they were one.

Rafiq reached over to open the drawer of the nightstand and remove a foil package.

"Come here, baby," he said, "help me put this on."

He'd already begun shielding himself. Using her mouth, Desiree helped him finish the job. After rolling her onto her side, he gently entered her from behind. Then, wrapping his arms around her, he pressed her along the length of him and began to move in a sensuous rhythm.

Rafiq's palm's slid along the surface of her breasts. He rolled a nipple between his thumb and index finger and let the heat intensify. She was burning up and close to exploding. Rafiq's grunts signaled he wasn't far behind her.

Any inhibitions she'd ever had left her. Desiree was no longer conscious of the room, just the man inside her. As Rafiq's thrusts intensified, she matched him move for move.

"Come with me, baby," he said giving one last gigantic thrust and bringing her close to the edge.

Her throbbing body exploded. Wide-eyed, open-mouthed, and no longer capable of logical thought, she gave in to the sensations flooding her.

CHAPTER 22

Two days later, Desiree was seated in a restaurant in Washington, D.C., waiting for Terrence to show up. She spotted him almost immediately as he made his way to her table. Her brother's carriage could not be ignored. He stalked rather than walked and, as always, he was impeccably dressed.

Desiree raised her hand acknowledging his almost imperceptible nod.

She'd gotten to D.C. way before the appointed time. Not in a financial position to shop, she'd passed the time strolling on Pennsylvania Avenue and stopping to gaze at the White House, fascinated by the place that housed the movers and shakers of the United States.

"How was the ride down?" Terrence greeted, taking the seat opposite her.

"Not bad at all. I hardly hit traffic. How was your flight?"

"Uneventful. A few bumps, but nothing to speak of."

He gazed around the restaurant, appearing pleased at the setting. It had been his choice and perfect for a business lunch. Shelves of books lined the walls. It clearly catered to the powerful and well-heeled, the deal makers of Washington, D.C.

"Shall we order?" Terrence asked, glancing at his Baume and Mercier. Desiree wondered if there was ever a time when he relaxed.

A polished waiter took their order and disappeared. He returned a short time later bearing their food on platters covered by domes.

When Desiree was done with her Cobb salad and Terrence had inhaled his shrimp wrap, he sat back in his chair.

"You must be wondering why I suggested we meet," he said.

Desiree figured she'd been summoned to discuss their father's estate. Not that she was expecting to be left anything. She'd relinquished any hope of an inheritance when she walked out.

"You mentioned business in D.C. Since I live close by, I figured you saw this as the perfect opportunity to catch up. How's Mom? Tanya?"

"Both are doing okay. How are things with you?"

"Fine...well, not so fine." What the hell—might as well tell him. "I'm job hunting, and that's not going well. I've landed nothing at all."

Terrence seemed visibly perplexed. He brushed an imaginary crumb from a spotless white cuff. "Hmm. I thought you were teaching. Aren't you happy where you are?"

"I was happy until I got fired."

Terrence's shirt no longer held his interest. He looked her squarely in the face. "People normally aren't fired without reason. What did you do?"

How to tell him? Desiree decided being vague was best. She took a deep breath and began. "A past indiscretion surfaced, something I'm not particularly proud of. Just one of those things."

Terrence hiked an eyebrow. How on earth had she acquired such a stuffy brother? She'd better explain.

"I applied for a promotion, one I was fairly certain I might get, then out of the blue a video that had been taken of me a long time ago was sent to the dean of my school."

"Hmm," Terrence said again, appearing deep in thought. "I wonder if it's a copy of the same video I'm here to discuss."

Now he had her full attention. "What video? Where did you find it?"

Terrence told her all about packing up her father's study and discovering the locked cabinet.

"Who would have thought the old man had been keeping tabs on you all these years?" Terrence said. "Imagine the expense of having a private eye on retainer."

Desiree didn't give a good gosh darn. It seemed an invasion of privacy to her. "He shouldn't have wasted his time," she said heatedly.

"Obviously he cared about your well-being."

"Then he had a funny way of showing it. There were times when I almost starved to death. Did you see the video?"

Terrence's visible start was sure confirmation.

"Yes, the contents were disturbing. It was hard to believe you would prostitute yourself."

So he thought she'd sold out. Easy for him to pass judgment. He'd not been in a bind. He'd had money and a decent place to live.

"We do lots of things we regret," Desiree said, choosing her words carefully. "Some out of necessity." Then it came to her with the force of lightning. "Do you think Father, having kept track of me, could have sent that video off to the school? What would he have hoped to achieve?"

One of Terrence's large hands circled the glass of iced tea. "No, he would have been too ill. It was Tanya. I confronted her."

Tanya, the older sister she'd once worshipped. "You are kidding! Tell me you are."

"I'm afraid not. She actually confessed. She had a key to that cabinet. Father trusted her implicitly. When he fell ill, she was feeling put-upon. She needed you home to help with his care."

"And sending that video was supposed to get my attention? My own sister ruined me."

Terrence gulped his iced tea and set the almost-empty glass down. "I was pretty much estranged from the family, so she couldn't count on me. Tanya made a calculated move. She sent that tape to your school knowing that it would wreak havoc. If you were fired, you would then be free to come home. You'd help care for our father."

Desiree was slowly beginning to understand her sister's illogical reasoning. "But I hadn't been in touch with the family in years," she cried. "What if I didn't give a damn?"

"You could easily have adopted that attitude, but Tanya counted on your compassion. She thought you'd come home, jobless and desperate."

"But why not play on your sympathy? You were closer." Desiree pointed out.

"Because I made it clear I hated the old man. He was awful to mother. It's no secret I wanted him dead."

How could her own flesh and blood be that cruel? And to think she'd suspected first Rafiq and then Conrad. She'd been wrong on both counts; the heinous act had been performed by a woman Desiree thought had the world on a string.

"My own sister. It's hard to believe."

"Coffee?" Terrence asked, already signaling to the

waiter. In seconds two cups appeared. Terrence remained silent as the waiter poured.

Terrence waited for the man to leave before picking up the threads of the conversation. "According to Tanya, she tried reaching you numerous times. You never returned any of those calls."

"I don't know why she bothered. The damage was done once she sent off that tape."

"Do you need money?" Terrence asked abruptly.

Desiree's jaw set. She stared off into the distance. Desperate as she was beginning to get, no way would she accept her brother's charity.

"Something will break eventually." she muttered.

"I'm in a position to help," Terrence offered. "I mean that. I can lend you money. I don't want you to repeat a foolish mistake."

Desiree decided it would be best to subtly change the subject. What was done was done. There was nothing she could do to change it. She would manage. She always had.

"We'd like to make you an offer," Juliet Hoffman, the principal of the Chesapeake school, said when Desiree got on the line.

Desiree's palm covered the mouthpiece. "Yes!" Finally. She kept the other on the wheel, making sure the car didn't swerve into the far lane. Someone was finally willing to hire her.

"Desiree," Juliet repeated. "Are you there? Did you hear me? We want you on our faculty and we are willing to offer a competitive salary. Do you need time to think about this?"

"Uh, yes, I do, and thank you. I'll get back to you in a day or two?"

"Good. I'll be waiting to hear."

Desiree thanked Juliet again before disconnecting. Slowly it began to penetrate. She had a job. Of course she would accept. It wasn't as if there were other employers beating down her door. To date, she'd had a phone interview with Monmouth College and no return call.

The offer was all she could think of as she drove to Rafiq's. She couldn't wait to tell him. But would he be delighted for her? They'd both hoped Monmouth College would come through.

Desiree sobered immediately, thinking about how this job offer could affect her and Rafiq. Chesapeake and New Jersey weren't that far apart, and he'd said they'd somehow make it work. But long-distance relationships were rough and had a poor survival rate.

No, she would not think of it. This was cause to celebrate. Glancing out the window, she was amazed at the greenery. Summer was truly here. Where had the time gone?

She had no other option but to accept the job. Now what to do with her house? Should she rent or sell?

As Desiree pulled up, she spotted Rafiq pulling weeds in the garden. He was versatile, all right, easily going from Mr. Scholastic to athletic stud overnight. And even though his shorts had seen better days, the formfitting T-shirt molded to his muscular chest made her want to devour him.

"Hey, babe," he greeted as she sailed through the gate. "You look like you won the lottery. What's that smile about?"

"I got a job," she said, hugging him. "I actually got an offer."

He picked her up and spun her around. "That's great. Who with?"

She knew he was hoping she would be moving to Monmouth County with him.

"The school in Chesapeake," she said, knowing she was bursting his bubble. "They're the first to make me an offer."

"Oh, baby, that's great, definite cause to celebrate. Let's drink to your success. What will it be? Juice, water or some other concoction?"

As she'd expected, he wasn't entirely elated. His tone was a little off. Desiree followed him into the kitchen and watched him inspect the fridge.

"I have the fixings for Bloody Marys or mimosas?" he said the minute his head popped out.

"I'll drink whatever you're having," she answered, wrapping her arms around his waist.

His head disappeared inside the refrigerator again as he grabbed two bottles of water. He stood and handed one to her.

Rafiq's forced smile said it all. His eyes no longer held their usual sparkle.

"Why do I get the feeling you're not happy for me?" Desiree asked.

"Am I that transparent?"

"Umm-hmm."

Rafiq took a step toward her, closing the distance between them. "I'd hoped we'd be working together."

Desiree's hand stroked his cheek. "I know, babe. But I have bills to pay. I can't turn this down."

He huffed out a breath. "I'd like to be in the position to say, 'Take a chance. Come with me to New Jersey. We'll worry about you working when we get there.'"

"I know. I know.'

Rafiq's index finger worried his chin. It was a cute gesture and one that she loved. "How about you do this? Call Monmouth College and tell them you have an offer—that might hurry things along."

"I will." Desiree let him embrace her. She inhaled the familiar scent of soap along with the pungent soil. She would miss him, this man that she'd come to love.

His hands slid under her shirt, kneading her flesh. When Rafiq kissed her, the kitchen and every mundane problem ceased to exist.

They would work it out somehow.

CHAPTER 23

"Your credentials are certainly impressive. We would love to have you as part of the team," the man who'd lobbed questions at her for almost an hour finally said.

Desiree let the words sink in. She'd followed up on Rafiq's suggestion and contacted Monmouth College. That call must have prodded them out of inertia, because she'd been invited to come up to New Jersey for a second interview. She'd never expected to be offered a job on the spot.

"What about relocation expenses?" she finally had the presence of mind to ask.

"I'm afraid we can't offer that, but we do have affordable faculty housing on campus. And we pay a competitive salary, not to mention good benefits."

Two job offers in the space of one week.

"What are we talking about in terms of salary?" Desiree asked, figuring it was safe to ask since the dean had brought it up.

He named a salary range that exceeded her expectations, then stood. "You can discuss our benefits with Kendra from Human Resources." Dean Mueller glanced over at the woman whom he'd summoned toward the end of their talk. He extended his hand.

Desiree shook it in shock. She was still unable to believe her luck. She could be with the man she loved. They could begin to plan a life together.

"You two talk," the dean said as he left them.

For another fifteen minutes she listened to the HR woman, who'd introduced herself as Kendra Allen, discuss benefits.

Not wanting to appear too anxious, she kept her voice modulated while asking questions, although, as far as she was concerned, the decision was made. Who in their right mind would turn down this opportunity? The salary was more than she'd ever dreamed possible and benefits included tuition.

"I think we've covered everything." Kendra Allen handed over her card. "Please call me if you have further questions."

Together they walked to the door. Dean Mueller was waiting outside. Desiree thanked him for the interview and walked out into a perfect summer day, made even more perfect by the unexpected job offing. She'd thought for sure that a third interview might be in the making. Practically skipping, she headed for the rental car. The forty-minute drive to Newark airport didn't seem that daunting anymore.

She had a job. Wait until she told Rafiq.

Three weeks later Desiree was wedged into the passenger seat of Rafiq's SUV. The vehicle was stacked to the roof with boxes. Much of their stuff had been sent ahead, including her car, which would be delivered by a transportation service.

Renting the condominium had been easy. Zinga, whose lease had come to an end, had gleefully agreed to move in. She'd even accepted the place furnished.

"Ready?" Rafiq asked, putting the vehicle in gear and patting Desiree's bare leg where her shorts had crept up.

She tugged on the hem of her shorts and slapped at his hand. Resting her head on the seat back she contemplated it all. "Am I ever. I'm looking forward to starting a whole new life."

"The best," he said, sliding her hand into his.

She knew she'd made the right decision. She was finally free of secrets. She'd even told Dean Mueller about her stint as an actress and why she had made that awful video. He'd remained unfazed. It had taken years, but she could finally live her life without shame.

And just yesterday, Tanya, probably coerced by Terrence, had called to apologize. Desiree had accepted her apology. There was no point in holding on to a grudge. Good things had actually resulted from her being fired. She had a developing relationship with a man who respected her and thought she was special.

Sandi, getting wind of Desiree's good fortune, had also phoned, bubbling over with her own news, of course. She and Glenn Browne were getting along, but even so, she had decided to move on. In a few weeks she would be leaving for Los Angeles to audition for a part she'd heard about.

Desiree had wished her well. She'd decided that she was as much to blame as Sandi for all that had transpired. She'd relinquished her power and allowed fear to take over. She'd let Sandi run over her.

Rafiq was the one that mattered now. Since he didn't consider her less of a person for giving up her child, why would she care what others thought? This man, this wonderful man, reminded her repeatedly that her decision had been the right one. He'd promised her that if she ever felt the urge to find her daughter, he'd do all in his power to make that happen.

And Byron well, Byron, in a last-ditch effort to get her back, had come to the condo declaring his love. She'd sent him packing. Cutting that tie had been a liberating and satisfying experience. It confirmed she'd really moved on.

"What are you thinking about, baby?" Rafiq asked

when they were on the highway. "You've got a smile on your face rivaling the Mona Lisa's."

Desiree draped an arm around his neck. "I'm thinking how lucky I am to have you."

"Luck has little to do with it." Rafiq took his eyes off the road for a second and smiled back at her. "It was destiny. Fate sent you to me. Look at all the wonderful things that happened since we hooked up. We're moving to a new place. We both have jobs. You helped me find an agent who's interested in my book. Life couldn't be better."

"Oh, yes, it could."

"What do you mean?" he asked, a troubled look on his face.

"We could have that baby you once mentioned."

There was a pause. Rafiq's expression quickly changed. Gone was the light mood. "Is this your way of telling me you're pregnant?" he asked.

"Not yet. But I plan to work at it."

He steered the car off to the side of the road, quickly parked, and took her into his arms.

"You would consider having my baby?"

"Of course I would."

"Even though there's a chance that child might suffer from bipolar disorder?"

"Why not? You said it yourself in your book. The disease is manageable if diagnosed early and treated with the proper medication."

"Baby, you're wonderful," he said, kissing her cheek. "Here's what we'll do. We'll discuss the possibility in six months, after we get settled. We'll talk about getting married and having our baby."

Desiree's jaw dropped. Rafiq had just declared himself. He was offering her much more than she dared even hope for.

"You're proposing to me?" she asked.

"Damn right I am."

Before she could say another word he kissed her passionately.

"So what do you say?" Rafiq asked when they separated.

"Yes, of course!"

"I am one lucky man."

He put the car back in gear and drove off.

As they left Bethesda behind, Desiree got to thinking about life on the whole. Here she was, on top of the world. She now had everything she wanted.

After what seemed a lifetime of living a lie, she had found the perfect love.

He was perfect for her and it seemed life didn't get any better than this.

Dear Reader,

Life happens whether we want it to or not, although how we handle adversity is crucial. It's all in attitude, I say. Do we become crippled, or do we say lesson learned, brush ourselves off and move on?

Like Desiree, most of us have been devastated by a friend's betrayal. Most pick themselves up and move on. The resilient and healthy chalk it up to lessons in life and emerge far better people. Some allow paralysis to set in and grow more and more bitter.

As a daughter of an educator, I have a high regard for teachers. I've also spent way too many years in the corporate world, and am familiar with intrigue and corporate maneuvering.

That said, I hope you enjoy *Shattered Images,* and that you find it both inspiring and uplifting. If so, please feel free to e-mail me at Mkinggamble@aol.com or write me at P.O. Box 25143, Fort Lauderdale, FL 33320. A stamped, self-addressed envelope will ensure a response. You may also keep in touch through my Web site www.lovemarcia.com.

Thank you for your support and remember to keep reading.

Best,

Marcia King-Gamble